THE ITALIAN ACTRESS

excelsior editions

AN IMPRINT OF STATE UNIVERSITY OF NEW YORK PRESS

THE ITALIAN ACTRESS

a novel

FRANK LENTRICCHIA

Published by
state university of new york press, albany

© 2010 State University of New York

For information, contact
State University of New York Press, Albany, NY
www.sunypress.edu

Production and book design, Laurie Searl
Marketing, Fran Keneston

Library of Congress Cataloging-in-Publication Data

Lentricchia, Frank.
The Italian actress : a novel / Frank Lentricchia.
p. cm.
ISBN 978-1-4384-3044-7 (pbk. : alk. paper)
1. Motion picture producers and directors—Fiction.   2. Actresses—Fiction.
3. Americans—Italy—Fiction.   4. Italy—Fiction.   I. Title.

PS3562.E4937I83 2010
813'.54—dc22   2009022699

10 9 8 7 6 5 4 3 2 1

for **Fred Jameson**

I

CLAUDIA

 It was there, in Volterra, that I found them: the fantastically named Sigismondo Malatesta and his companion of a thousand devious allures, who called herself Isotta degli Atti. It was in Volterra—Tuscany's most forbidding walled city of stone—at an obscure festival—the only kind that invites me now. In that harsh place, where I won no prize for continuing achievement in video, or any other prize, at the villa of an aging Italian film star (female, divorced, rich, beautiful still, and available) who said, it was Claudia, actually Claudia, and she said—violent thunder and lightning breaking over the mountains, driving the guests from her garden and leaving the two of us standing alone and too close in sudden dark, awaiting rain—and Claudia at that moment said in her fatal, raucous voice, "Jack, you cannot win a prize because you are in your own self the prize. Am I old enough to be your mother? *Sì, certo!* Do we care? Are you afraid? Speak to me. Why don't you speak?" I laughed in a certain way, because I could not speak. I finally summoned words. I said, stupidly, "Thank you, Claudia," and she replied, "Is that what you want to do, Jack? To thank me? What have I given?"

3

In her vicinity, I tended to shortness of breath. I thought of this woman as I thought of the work I hadn't been doing for so long and the work I wanted yet to do: it's not going to happen, because passion is a word in a language I had long since ceased to understand, if ever I did. (Do I care that she is old enough to be my mother? I have yet to decide.)

My name is Jack Del Piero, former avant-garde videographer, long detached—without regret—from my Italian-American origins. If you wish, you may gloss "former avant-garde" as "last week's wilted salad," or—should you be of brutal disposition—call me "garbage," on the menu still and a favorite with those of nostalgic appetite. I'm also a periodic stutterer who would sing with all the notes connected, as in a single breath, but fluency is a river I'll not swim in: better to write than to talk.

Twenty years ago, my silent videos won special prizes at Taormina and Venice for their "radical experiments in pornography and the beauty of their images." *Osservatore Romano* pronounced my soul an abomination. "His actors," wrote the reviewer for *Le Monde*, "are at all times fully clothed. Never do they touch, one another, or themselves, but the erotic charge is unbearable. What exactly is *done* in Mr. Del Piero's disturbing art is unspeakable in public print, even in Paris."

In the mirror of my videos I banish disaster; I banish myself. There, and nowhere else, I find myself a figure of surpassing grace and savage wit, handsome even; my father's son at last. But at the time I met her—Claudia—I hadn't made a video in twenty years; I'd reverted to being inescapable Jack Del Piero.

They invited me to Volterra (at Claudia's urging, she revealed much later) for the same reason I was invited to all the marginal festivals: as an ironic example for the idealistic young—I mean the attractive, the fresh-faced, the energetic, the goddamn young—a blasted figure of purity and poverty I am, out of the past, salt-and-pepper hair to the shoulders, lean and hard at 48 (I grow old), and apparently not unappealing, if I can trust Claudia. I suppose I mean, see myself through her eyes, which I cannot.

In Volterra, I served as bitter inspiration for the up-and-comers who'd one day receive, perhaps they'd receive, once or twice, no more than that, glancing—barely glancing—notice at festivals more questionable even than the one at Volterra and who would attempt to assuage themselves to the grave with my memory, thinking of themselves, absurdly, as artistic kin, as having once made it to my level before disappearing, like me, into romantic obscurity—not able ever to think of themselves truthfully (an infinitely excusable fault) as among the legion of artists who were, from the beginning, forever down, and out of sight, and never romantic.

Meeting me, Malatesta said that night at Claudia's, was like meeting the immensely gifted fifth bassoonist of the London Philharmonic, third cousin of John Lennon, whose name (the fifth bassoonist's) would remain forever on the tip of the tongue, never to be recalled, never to be spoken. "Until now," he said: "and here you are, Jack, face to face in Volterra and they are eager to talk with someone else. They are so embarrassed for you and for themselves, especially for themselves, because they do not wish to be near you, they have no interest, they cannot withstand your putrefying presence and who can blame them? (Though Isotta and I are drawn to it: your putrefaction.) You are the mirror of their future. You are invited here to teach them who they are. *Caro mio*, I must tell you that Isotta and I have a plan. Without you, we cannot tell our story; the plot fails." Isotta added, "In Rimini, you work as you like, or waste time as you like." Sometime later, I asked Malatesta how many bassoonists were seated in the London Philharmonic. He replied, "Four."

I take late coffee and oranges and too many *cornetti* (marmalade-infused) on her wind-swept veranda, with a view to the walled and towered city, her olive orchard spilling below me silver and green down the hill into the deep-clefted and awful gorge that separates villa and Volterra—a mile across as the crow flies—the city high on its imperious throne of rock. Volterra is medieval old, cold and grim—a uniform world of gray stone—no trees, no flowers, no shrubs, no grass—a paradise of the inorganic, of death—and deeply, deeply comforting to contemplate, the object of this would-be ascetic's desire. In opposition—these were my every morning's choices—there she is, before me in the heated pool, calling out as I meditate on my fiftieth birthday, as I grow fat about the middle in my second year with her, my second year of pregnancy (I am big with Claudia). She, the subversion of my tranquility—my icy dream of Volterra—she, that sumptuous and supple body, brown and naked, afloat in liquid turquoise. "Jack," she says, she laughs, "I like you with your new belly. Tonight I make the ponytail. Now you must for me jump in and join my pleasure. Quick, *caro*, take off your clothes." The raucous voice says "pleasure," but promises delights not exclusively, or even predominantly, erotic.

She says that she is the solution. She says that we are the story. She says that so-called Sigismondo and Isotta (those appalling mountebanks) are not the story. I tell her that I disagree. I tell her so often, and she replies just as often, and always the same, that it is preferable to choose simplicity: "my bed," she says, "and wild boar steak, the tomatoes heavy from the vine and the basil and the figs, the figs big like pears, I pick them for you, they are warm still, like me, from the sun, and warm more from the hands that pick them. Touch my hand, Jack, before it is too late. Your hands are cold. Jump in and lose your brains."

I did not jump in; I'm not one to jump in. I talked. Even now, with some understanding of who the man is who writes this, as he remembers, I wouldn't change the words that I'd say to her—if I could say them to her now, as I said them then. Words hidden in me, day and night: When I saw you first in "8½," Claudia, in white, the day itself a bowl of white, you came gliding over the grass—do you remember?—your smile sailed me in a surround of white sky and I couldn't tell you from the radiance, you were the embodied radiance as you came to Marcello in his fantasy—I was there, I was the unseen fantasist as you descended to minister to the faulty instincts of our manhood. Did the jaded crew prick up its ears and stare?

Later, in that scene in the hotel room, where our desire summoned you in chiaroscuro, you and I and Marcello in salacious complicity to betray the Angel of Mercy, you smoothed the bedsheets, terrifying us in your slip, then turned, lubricious, to the camera's gaze (I was the camera) radiant still but darkly so in the blood light of eros. You came as someone else—who are you really, Claudia?—you came to minister to the needy again, but for a different kind of need. Do you remember?

This is how she responded to my moon-struck rhapsody: First with a kind laugh. Then this: "It is only the light design; it is only the cinematografia; it is only the acting, though it does not please me to call it acting. Because I am in Fellini only a volume of space, like a tree, or chair, but more flexible. Are you hearing me? The films are false. You have the chance to destroy the lies of my mystery. But you make more mystery. In the scenes you talk about I do not speak; I am only a body. But I speak. Who am I really? Before I go to bed or to make love I go to the toilet. Are you understanding me? I am here. Are you here? Come, jump in and I will make you real." I don't tell her that, unlike you, Claudia, Volterra is hard, Volterra repels—and that's why I'm drawn to it.

7

I sat on her veranda in all kinds of weather because I believed that the sick improve (I do not say get well) in the open air. I contracted my ills when I left Claudia—not reluctantly—for an extended period, to work in Rimini and to play a considerable role in the plot of Sigismondo and Isotta. The point of Rimini was work: I was working again, I was going to look in the mirror of my new video and pronounce myself the man I wanted to be. These ills of mine, I admit, are in part mental, or—as my father was fond of saying to me in my teen years—"only mental." My father found himself—on occasion—mildly funny, and so did I.

Claudia says it's easier to choose life and that only the mad overcome the difficulty of the choice for death. I am not mad, she assures me. She says I am sad (no rhyme in Italian) and must embrace the sadness *con tutta la tua forza*, with all your power. If I do that, then I shall embrace her for our good remaining days on this terrible earth. "You desire to embrace me, Jack, though you do not." She insists it's best to choose the easy course because the end will be hard enough and reassures me (reassurance being her most reiterated speech act) that I am safe now. "In my house," Claudia says, "we are not actors; it is not permitted."

I believed it possible that I'd recover; believed this especially when she took me riding in her vintage '65 Mustang, meticulously restored, on narrow roads, top down over hills blanketed with vineyards and a countryside dominated by islands of noble cypresses and the occasional ochre-colored villa. We avoid the obvious: Siena and Florence. We work, but fail to skirt the difficulty between us as we take the narrowest of side roads, lanes really—the vegetation and overhanging trees virtually closing off the passage in places, brushing the sides of the car—where we are at last free of careening

Italian motorcyclists. We stop here and there awhile in forgotten villages—no tourists, no art treasure—villages of a single café on a desolate little piazza where we take a macchiato and sweet around eleven and, at four, a small sandwich of salami and provolone, with Campari on the rocks, at a table on the piazza, under a canopy, during sudden showers interrupted by sudden shafts of sun, the light brilliant on the ruined façade across the way. We take our pleasure in the food and drink and each other: in this latter, she vocally, me in silence.

I tell her she is the sudden shaft of sunlight, I the more than intermittent shower, the too often all-day downpour, and she replies, "Yes, we go together like prosciutto and cold melon." Then one time I blurt it out, I say, "Let's tell the truth, Claudia, I've been living with you for two years, more or less, and we have yet to make love. I point to the ruined façade and say, I am that ruined façade." She says, "Not in my house, this ruined façade; you make too much drama." She says, "Anticipation is good." (Sigismondo's favorite line.)

Apropos of nothing, I tell her that my parents cared dearly for me, my childhood was not tragic, but they cared for one another even more, perhaps too much more and for this sin of passion they carried guilt for me and self-loathing, they carried these things like old broken-down pack horses dying of thirst in the desert and needing the mercy of a sudden bullet in the brain. She says, "Today you talk pretty again like the writers I do not read." I tell her that my mother got what she needed: a massive coronary, out of the blue—she who had no family history of such problems hit the floor like a ton of bricks. My father also got what he wanted: the flair of a theatrical big finish—Wagnerian *Liebestod*. Claudia says we will not endure such problems, because she is too old to give birth "and if you wait much longer to make love to me, I will be under the earth. No children, no guilt, no loathing of ourselves, but the sadness, of course. It is possible a big heart attack. Why not? But Wagner? No Wagner in my house and the only Verdi we are permitting is *Falstaff*. Because it is better to be *buffoni*, the two of us, but especially you, Signor Melodrama. And the Beatles, *sì*: I love you yeah yeah yeah." (I fail to withhold a grin.)

I say, "I'm going to do it, I'm going to edit the Rimini video." She says, "In my house?" "I'll go public with this horror," I say, "I'm coming back strong at Taormina, I'll take it all the way to Cannes." She says, "If you wish; I do not wish. Do you wish, Jack, in your secret heart?" I say, "I don't know. Only The Shadow knows." "In my house," she laughs, she says, "shadows are not permitted."

So it goes: touring the Tuscan hills, chatting in lonely cafés. Or much reading (me) and much gardening (she). Claudia reads little. She keeps house, not because she doesn't want to spend for help but because she likes it. Soccer is an addiction: she is an Italian. She says that when Roberto Baggio missed the penalty kick in overtime at the World Cup she became "scarred for life." She watches the soccer channels in the afternoon and is teaching me to understand this beautiful game, beautiful (like Claudia) even when I do not understand. These are our days. Our nights: We cook together. She's good, but soon, she says, I'll be better. And it's probably true. I have the touch, but not the experience. Or the will. We go to bed in separate rooms, without submerged rancor. There is no rancor.

After two years I'm making some progress: I'm almost used to looking at her; I share a villa with one of the world's most stunning women and I'm possibly on the blessed road to ordinariness. Getting over her looks is not really the problem. (Well, somewhat of a problem.) It's getting over the way she takes me in; the obvious (even to me) pleasure she takes in my company (even my long silences). From the beginning she's behaved as if we've known each other forever, and it's no act: "Not in *casa mia*, although you,

Jack, sometimes make operas out of yourself." It's the quality of her attention and it's difficult, maybe impossible, for me to accept that I could be the object of that gaze, that she is not suffering from some temporary hallucination which, once it passes—you complete the thought. When I sense that my capitulation is near, I tell her that I am my father's son. This is my final line of defense. I remind her of how he went out, that passion is the royal road to self-destruction. She only says, "What was your father's name? It was Frank, yes? Is your name Frank? Are you changing your name to Frank? No? Why not? I am closing the case. *Basta*, Jack." (A week ago, I held her hand.)

Claudia is candid, improbably unaware of her charm, but not unaware—how could she be?—of her beauty: "I am beautiful, they say, but what can it matter when we eat breakfast together with bad breath after 2,000 days?" Only the truly unaffected can smile as she does. Above all, she is unpredictably exciting. On that first night in Volterra she brushed aside my comments about her films, took my hand and led me to the vast garage to show me an ancient Mercedes engine, laid out in what seemed to me, but not to her, a chaos of pieces, small and large, on a grease-stained floor. With the enthusiasm of a teenage boy, she was learning automechanics from a forbidding technical manual, also grease-stained: the kind of book, she said, that she enjoyed. The following morning—that is, the morning after the first of many chaste nights at the villa—she took me to an outdoor market and pointed out that all the customers were women because women must do these things, but she, who has many euros to hire servants, goes to market twice a week because the sight of fresh produce and the odor of fresh bread lifts the fallen flesh—this said with a frank glance downward to her wondrous chest. It pleases her to tell me at the fish market that her brother, professor of cinema in Palermo, upon hearing of her interest many years ago in my infamous videos, had summarized for her the ideas of a still landmark study of my importance to the field, the international bestseller *The Pornographics of Everyday Life: Notes on the Structure of Postmodern Beauty*. It was fortunate that Renato had explained this difficult thinking (which drew her closer to the idea of me before we met—closer, she said, than even these excellent stinks of fish) because she herself was not capable of reading such a book. She said that many "bombs of sex" from the movies, "like poor Marilyn," wish to be valued for their minds, that she had been one of those big bombs, she too had a mind, but it was not a mind in the sense that Renato and the other bombs meant this word of the intellectual class. She said that if we should value each other, it would be for everything we absorbed from "the eyes, the ears, the hands and the mouth, especially the tongue, because this is how healthy people find the spirit and the mind, there is no other way, *caro mio*, I do not want to be loved for my so-called mind alone."

When Claudia speaks, I am almost composed. (Yesterday, I touched her shoulder.)

I treat her to my reflections on minor Italian cities. I say, "Maybe I'll do a career change and become a travel writer."

She replies, "Can you do this and not leave Volterra again?"

I tell her that tourists demand Florence, Siena, and the territory between—"the Chianti region, where hills and cozy valleys are fluently intertwined—like fortunate lovers," I say, tactlessly; "where you become the measure of an intimate world, the vital center of space and time. Where you feel safe."

"Can you touch me now? In my vital center? I want to feel safe."

"In Volterra, the land falls disastrously away, undermined by obscure forces that create a desolate terrain of cliffs. On the long approach to the city, as you traverse the way to the top, all is steeply eroded: in spring not a wild flower blooms."

"This is not true," Claudia says. "I have seen two wild flowers."

"The view from outside Volterra's walls is of five disturbing valleys, without end. Mist blurs the outlines of all objects—form deteriorates into formlessness, the insecure. You are not the center; there is no center; you feel an encroaching terror."

"But what do you truly fear? I do not believe that it can be Volterra. *Tesoro*, I, also, have fear, but not of Volterra."

"With the exception of one building, Rimini is of no interest. For the thousands who in summer invade from Germany and the Scandinavian countries, touring and gazing is never the object. They don't come because they recall Rimini as the city of Fellini's birth and the subject of two of his films. They have heard the name Fellini, but have not seen the films. Many, in fact, are no doubt of the assured opinion that Fellini is a variety of pasta, short and wide."

"When you have truly recovered from your illness, you will be kinder and not make such cruel jokes. You will not fear to be kind."

"Nor do those northern invaders, dear Claudia, come in the hot months because they remember and are drawn by the singular name of Rimini's legendary and lethal ruling family—Malatesta, the name that conjured fear and hatred in the thirteenth, the fourteenth, the fifteenth centuries. They have no need, as I did, to stalk narrow, cobbled streets, seeking contact where once he, Sigismondo, strolled in outrageous arrogance—he, the most shocking of Malatesta scions, the original Sigismondo, Renaissance soldier of fortune, and bloody visionary who caused the Tempio Malatestiano to be erected as a monument to himself and his passion for Isotta degli Atti, the third wife. He loved her to distraction."

"Maybe it made him happy to be distracted."

"He invited Piero della Francesca to Rimini to live and paint in his castle and diddle his servants of both sexes, if he so wished. I was seeking contact with this Sigismondo, said to have murdered his first two wives in order to clear the path for Isotta, to whom he'd lost himself. Sometimes, he'd written to her, a few weeks before his death, with these Popes and Cardinals it is required that with my knife I go in."

"I think you care for this dead man. Are you in love?"

"They come to Rimini for the sun, the beaches of white sand, the warm and murky Adriatic."

"Are you in love?"

"They come in hopes of an unforgettable encounter with an astonishing (if unemployed) Italian, and they are not denied."

"I am an unemployed Italian—formerly astonishing."

"In winter, Rimini is a ghost town—battered by gale-force winds off the sea, fog-enshrouded, cold and damp. Especially in winter, I found Rimini irresistible."

After I've finished treating her to my dyspeptic ruminations, Claudia responds, fiercely, "Is it possible that you are writing a travel book for malcontents? Why do you make these comparisons? Why is it necessary to make comparisons of these places, if you are truly content to be living where you are, with me, in Volterra, which you say that you prefer? If you so much prefer it to be here, near my body—this is my body, Jack—why must you say it so much that it is better for you to be here, with me? Your color is not so good."

Those two in Rimini called regularly after I met them in Volterra—I refused their invitation many times, but finally, after three months with Claudia, in early December, I accepted "to make," as they put it, "something very rare." When I informed her that I'd be leaving for Rimini, for how long I didn't know, just as I didn't know if I'd ever be back, she said, "Do you know who these people are?" "Yes, I think they're frauds." "No, Jack, they are only actors." I said, "I'm going anyway." For reply, she made a large gesture—comic, very Italian, and untranslatable. Had she repeated it, I might never have left.

I know what my father would have said. Because hadn't he—chaired professor of Extreme Aesthetics at Princeton—already said it, memorably, many years before, in a scholarly journal? "We cannot physically desire a woman whom we perceive and contemplate as beautiful. If we attempt to make love to her, we fail, even if she comes eagerly to us in her naked glory. The idea of erotic love with a woman of beauty presents itself as an absurdity, as if we had been asked to pole vault over Mount Everest. I submit that the beautiful woman, *qua* beautiful woman, has never been made love to, not once, because, truly perceived and contemplated, beauty kills desire: it paralyzes the will and awakens us to the thought of soothing death."

Had my father's argument ended there, it wouldn't have stirred offended commentary. The "argument *qua* argument," as one of his condescending fellow philosophers put it, "amounts to a mildly provocative extension of Immanuel Kant and other ascetics of beauty." But in violation of academic protocols, my father insisted on inserting—in the words of one of his detractors—"the slovenly empirical, the shamelessly personal": a revelation that stunned the entire discipline. "My ceaseless desire for my wife," he wrote, "was ignited only after a lengthy spell of chastity, in the early years of our marriage—when the repetitious realities of domestic life had thoroughly worked their disenchanting and banalizing effects on her numinous beauty. Our first sexual contact—how good it was!—followed close upon her first thunderous seizure by flatulence. It was then that I embraced not only my wife but also her wisdom. She'd said, during the long dry spell, 'If beauty lies in the eye of the beholder, then I hope to fill your senses, periodically, with my various corruptions. Darling, you simply cannot fuck an angel, *qua* angel.' "

Jack, he'd have said, forget the films and photos and attend to Claudia on her sick bed, crawl right in there with her; kiss her before she's brushed her teeth in the morning; request, and pray to be granted, permission to accompany her to the toilet. Then be prepared, if you dare to do these things, for the onset of fierce desire. Have the courage to be human and you'll find her entirely desirable, if you love.

It was, of course, my father who introduced me to Claudia's great early films, screening them for me many times in my teen years, in order to guide me—deviously, according to his ironic method—but always, I must believe, with my best interests at heart—onto the hard path of my humanization, the path which in his case led to suicide. I was enthralled. I bought the tapes, then the DVDs; when broke, in my early twenties, and working at a video rental store, I skimmed the till for my needs: I bought a sixteen millimeter copy of "8½"; I bought the two books of photos, long out of print, published only in Italy, for steep prices; I instructed a rare book dealer to locate and purchase, no matter the price, a pristine copy—I insisted on pristine, only a pristine copy would satisfy me—of the May 1961 issue of *Esquire* magazine—I was five at the time of its publication—the issue that contained her most ravishing photo, though I, as Daddy would have predicted, was neither ravished nor wished to ravish. Instead, I hid her away in the museum—the mausoleum (that's better) of my mind, where I viewed and viewed again, times without number, her lonely image in melancholy space. I was with her there—in melancholy space—released, like her, from this world's contingencies and desires, living inside Claudia's secreted images, where we felt ourselves trying to elude the grip of nature's vicious plot.

Quickly it became vocation and avocation to nourish and indulge my intimate friend—melancholy—a gift (from whom?) that baptized me for art and formed the secret ground beneath my prize-winning videos. Claudia's films and photos belonged to a world I could not have experienced, but nevertheless had invented as memory. As if I had once, with her, been there, had always been there with her. As if it had all, inevitably and deliciously, slipped away from us, except for the retained images—traces of a bygone world, which I cherished more than present life itself.

My appearances at Italian film festivals were occasions to bring her image closer, endow it with local time and habitation. I thought of her as late afternoon light in certain Italian cities (so many) bleeding color; as changing tones of color in changing light (so many tones); as my lonesome impressions, gathered from deserted Italian streets, in autumn and winter, when the tourists have departed, and their loitering consorts, also departed, and gusts of rain swept the streets clean for me, the lone wanderer walking to no end. Most of all, she was the elongated beauty—have you seen Claudia's elegant neck?—of a piazza in Ortigia, at dusk, when the lights of ancient buildings come on to bury the dying light of day and a young girl plays alone a fantasy game of soccer—the booted white ball catching soft light while she sings out *Calcio! Mamma! Calcio!* In those Italian moments, in those Italian places,

I made memories of the present. In Volterra, to shield myself from the presence and present time of Claudia was my exacting vocation. To convert desire to memory was my master strategy, when desire was not, itself, already memory.

I know now why the original Sigismondo, whose streets in Rimini I walked, whose air I believed I'd breathed, whose death room in the Castle—so he named it, *camera della morta*, while he and Isotta lived there in the flush of hot youth—I envisioned myself asleep in that death room, deeply, restfully, where she and he had died—I understood why this intrepid man of action, in his sonnets for the living Isotta, needed to imagine her—make her an image, an untouchable work of art. The image is cold. He imagined her stone cold dead. Presented her the poems as his passion's best gift. I didn't know the body of the beloved—Claudia's body—but I knew intimately what Sigismondo knew, knew it well on the day I came back to her from Rimini, a year after the day we met.

II

MONDO SIGISMONDO

 With reluctance, I began in Volterra to entertain the idea of embracing, rather than resisting, the massive slow change and even slower bitter revocation of who I thought I was, twenty years before, when at twenty-eight I was assailed by three events that seem to me now to have been virtually simultaneous. There are times when I think of those events as three versions of the same: the death of my parents, the drying up of my desire to create new experiments in video, and the inexplicable decision, at the height of my renown, to accept a position at an elite small college in New England, in the Program for Theoretical Meditation on Film and Video, whose undislodegable chairman was none other than Fred Ozaki—"Big Fred," as he was known in the profession—built like a sumo wrestler and with the attendant appetites—the author of *The Pornographics of Everyday Life*, my champion. Ozaki had secured the backing of his balkanized colleagues for my appointment by telling them that it would be useful to have one practitioner of the art on the premises—just one—in order to remind themselves of where they, the commentators and theorists, stand in the world-historical hierarchy. Are your knee pads

in order? Relax, ladies (he was reported to have said: there were no women in the Program), he's someone you'll enjoy humiliating in your own little ways.

In the classroom, in dreadful weekly meetings of the Program's faculty, I found myself not one hundred percent indifferent and daydreaming away the snail-crawling minutes. I was, at times, strangely comfortable in the presence of company which I found, against all expectations, almost good. In the hallways and meetings I cultivated a comic style featuring sudden, unpredictable sallies of acerbic wit, often self-directed. My colleagues thought of me as an anarchic comedian whose company was not unwelcome, whose comments were periodically, if weirdly, to the point. They invited me to their homes, eager to feed me, introduce me to their children, dogs and needy spouses. Even the students—whom I found narcissistic to a degree that forever redefines the term—even the little bastards and I seemed a little grateful, at times, to have found each other. (Are you thinking birds of a feather?) And in Big Fred I'd made a special friend. At last, an older brother. I worried about his enormous weight, his blood pressure, his cholesterol, his numerous gastrointestinal fiascos, his chronic prostititis, his genetic predisposition to colon cancer and his "unprotected sexual tourism," as he called it, in Bangkok, Amsterdam, and Salt Lake City—Fred Ozaki was a fifty-five-year-old force of nature, a madman teetering on the brink of medical catastrophe. I imagined the Program secretary calling to tell me he was dead—and I was afraid.

The festival at Volterra was to conclude a week before the start of the fall semester. On my second day at Claudia's, I faxed Big Fred that I'd been hospitalized with a ruptured appendix, that widespread peritonitis and actual gangrene had been detected. The medical prognosis was grim; I could leave Volterra before the end of the year only at risk to my life. He promptly faxed in response that he understood and respected the artist's periodic need for truancy, and in consideration of my twenty years of meritorious service he'd see to it that I would continue to be paid, because I was entitled, "as we all are, Jack, to commit some modest measure of fraud—the institution is simply geared for it and at some level actually welcomes it. To blow off one's classes, pal, on a not exactly infrequent basis is, and ever shall be, the essential academic fringe benefit. But no need to bullshit me, bro, because you know I love you." He'd get me a leave for the fall—after that his hands were tied, his colleagues being eager to confiscate my position for a rising star with an unpublished, but much circulated, dissertation, *On the Strategic Irrelevance of Film and Video.*

I didn't care; I wouldn't return for the spring semester because teaching, like most things, mostly bored me. Oh no, Claudia did not bore: she excited and scared me—two good things—but there were times, in the unforgiving light of noon, or when she wore her hair up, that she seemed harmless and dishearteningly familiar—the wholesome nice-looking gal next door gone suddenly old, and a little desiccated. I feared that, if I stayed with her, after a while she'd just be my good buddy, a senior citizen at death's door—at times a bit boring—for whom I'd never develop what I required: the consistent pleasure of high-voltage romantic agony.

Claudia said that the usual way to Rimini was too difficult and offered to fly me there; I refused. She said she would drive me there; I said no. My way involved two buses and three trains. The path to my destination—I wanted to think destiny—needed to be arduous and painful. Because what could be the worth of art—or love, for that matter—that came without persistent suffering?

I never told Claudia that I had no intention of returning to Volterra—Claudia, who said twice, the week before I left, that she

23

was afraid. Nor did I tell Ozaki that I didn't give a damn about the position he'd worked hard to get me, or all the perks he'd shoveled me steadily under the table, like the hefty travel budget which greased my way to European festivals—Big Fred, who seemed impervious to the assaults of fear—who made others, though not me, afraid.

With at best six weeks of wherewithal to my name and no place to lay me down, I neared Rimini that gray day in December to begin work on a blank. I didn't have a clue; an impossible circumstance for a video artist, in this instance easily over-ridden by the temptation that was Sigismondo and Isotta; overridden, as it was phrased in my schoolboy catechism, by "the glamour of evil," which our godparents renounce on our infant behalf at baptism—renunciation that in my case never took.

I went to Rimini without the camera that had been lying for twenty years at the back of a dusty closet in Connecticut, the camera that had been the cold instrument of my passion. Claudia and Fred were committed to my care, but I'd put my trust in a mysterious stranger who said in our last conversation that none of my concerns would be a concern, he'd take care of me, he promised, and so, he said, without untoward suggestion, would Isotta, in her own way. I gave little or no thought at all to Fred and Claudia, my steadfast benefactors. On the way to Rimini, I imagined I was about to recover the golden time of my twenties, when I cultivated deep isolation—when contact served only to interrupt the tranquility I found in the process of work, in which I lost the self I never wanted to have. When I stepped off the train I believed for no good reason—because I needed to believe—that I was at last closing in on her. My sexy lost art was calling me back to her bed again.

But where were they? They were not to be found at the station upon my arrival. At the information booth, I posed the question to which I could expect no answer and the response was quick:

24

"Ah, *ma certo*, Sigi and Iso," this spoken with a practiced smile and a mixture of affection and condescension generally reserved for children, or those adults closer to us than we'd wish, who are forever unaware that they routinely embarrass themselves in public places, whose iron self-ignorance (who am I to talk, you say?) irritates, it gnaws, it causes us to want to give them pain for making us witnesses to their impregnable sense of self-worth. We are—I am—perhaps, only envious.

They—Sigi and Iso, as I too would come to call them—were known figures, personages, objects of speculation, gossip, resentment and desire: that special kind of public property we call "celebrity," a story the community would tell me over the months in bits and pieces. It may even have been a true story—if not true to the unascertainable facts then to the deepest of community needs—but neither of the two in question would comment on the fragments that came my way and that I'd set before them at the earliest opportunity, except to say that what I had heard was another "story of Rimini," by and about Rimini. I might remember that the subject of the first story of Rimini was Paolo and Francesca. That many of the details of their legend, immortalized by Dante, could not be verified, or were outrageously wrong. He said, "Did I know my Dante?" She said, "Dante lied." In the thirteenth century, Paolo and Francesca; in the fifteenth, the second story of Rimini, the legend of Sigismondo and Isotta. "About whom," she said, "many lies: much malice." "And now here you are, at last, Del Piero, in the twenty-first century to give to the world the as yet uncreated spectacle of the new Sigismondo and Isotta. We three will enter the memory of the world as Rimini's third legend of reckless passion—because we are privileged, as our predecessors were privileged, to have found the necessary artist—you, Jack, are the necessary artist, and the world is ready to be grateful. You know this. You have known this from the moment we met in Volterra. Legend, the life story of a saint. Have you been saintly? Have you been practicing denial?" His glance moved slowly down my body. He was delighted. He said, "How do you say it in your country? Does the bear do number two in the garden?" Suddenly solemn-faced, he said, "Embrace this inaugural moment of your greatness." I said, "I don't do pornography—of the usual kind." She replied, "We are not interested in pornography—of the usual kind."

I get ahead of myself. I want to skip all the in between. Why should I, who know all the bits and pieces about the two devils—why should I feed them to you, one at a time, at teasing intervals? I'll tell you now, all at once, what I learned from the Riminesi about the devils, who were not at the station—I mean inside the station, when I was inside. Who were not to be spied, waiting for me, happy, outside, at the cab stand, ready to shower me with rose petals. Who were not to be seen directly across the street, in front of the café called *Otto e Mezzo* ("8½," Claudia's film), the café adjacent to the bus stop for San Marino, where the child of the richest man in the province was run over, killed—and it was she (said the gossips) who bore the replacement, but until I saw the stretch marks—ugly purple vertical slashes across the abdomen—I couldn't believe (who could?) that she had borne a child.

When I exited the station, I was approached by a burly man in livery, who led me to a Rolls Royce. He said, "You are the man." I said, "How do you know?" He replied, "Irrelevant." I said, "Where are we going?" He said, "The Grand Hotel." I said, "I can't afford it, not even now in low season." He replied, "Why are you having concerns when there are no concerns?"

Over the weeks and months the voices of Rimini said that so-called Sigismondo and Isotta were high-end prostitutes, who on alternate weekends each serviced both genders. That at some point before they erupted without warning on foot—dirty, dreadfully clothed—at the Roman arch, where we saw them for the first time in our city, they had already changed their names to those absurd names nowhere to be found in Italy for hundreds of years—not even in the south, Signor Del Piero, the ludicrous south—and she, who works for a tour guide agency, who specializes in the Tempio Malatestiano, who has four languages, including Russian—she is certainly not an Italian, though she speaks with the grace and perfection heard only in our region—this tall blond—such legs—we have enjoyed them but once, at the pageant—this consort of the one who calls himself Sigismondo, who was overheard at Café Geloso to call her Nadia—he, the most handsome man in this city of handsome men, who speaks only the so-called Italian of the wretched of Sicily—Sicily is the south of the south—Sicilian is an inscrutable language like Chinese—Sicilians are not Italians: they are Africans—and we understand him with the gravest of difficulty, whom we also suspect to be an impostor—he is very dark—a playwright, an actor, a circus barker come here to change his luck as a bellhop at The Grand Hotel, where he plays with the richest homosexuals of Scandinavia, when not imagining a drama for us Riminesi who are to be their adoring audience and suckhole subjects—we despise them as our forefathers despised the original Sigismondo and Isotta, who squandered our revenues on dogs, outlandish clothes and ass-kissing artists and intellectuals whom they gathered and fed, clothed and housed and pimped for at their court, while our forefathers lived in stinking hovels on dirt streets of the ghetto, mixed in with Jews and dominated by their 100 roaming and marauding dogs, whose tons of shit our forefathers were made to cart daily away—those animals they were instructed to feed at their own expense, or else. The original Sigismondo—my Christ!—he was a military genius at fifteen, a mercenary captain of fame, the ruler of our backwater city-state who fought for the Milanese against the Venetians, who bought him off with marble, at which time he switched for Venice against Milan, then fought for the Milanese, who had marble too, against the Florentines and the Venetians, whom he bitched, then for the Florentines he fought, who knew where to find the marble, against Milan, for and against the Pope—who can keep track? He fought like ten devils in swamps with water up to his neck to keep the hounds off him. He nearly died in a ditch outside Ravenna and returned home blood-soaked, head to toe—he refused to wash because it was not his blood but that of his boss's enemies who—the enemies—would next year in the cold rain of January be his new employer. He dragged stolen marble by ox-drawn carts to Rimini—he yanked it violently out of cemeteries and churches. All for the magnificent Tempio, this treachery and bravery and cruelty. This was a man, a great and dreadful man, who given the need would do anything and, yes, we—you, too, Signor Del Piero, it is so obvious if you could only see your face now—we admire him, a man free to do whatever he pleases, whenever, even to butcher a wife. But this new Sigismondo, what is there to admire? And yet you keep his company like a brother, or shall we say lover? That Castel Sismondo, you will notice its battle stations face inward to the heart of the city because they feared our forefathers more than they feared that most ugly of men, Federico da Montefeltro of Urbino, who lacked Sigismondo's mind and violence and personal beauty but bested him in the end with superior cunning. We acknowledge his personal beauty, his love of learning, his love of violence, his passion for Isotta—the Tempio he built is one of the world's most melancholy artistic wonders, a monument to death, so they say—we have little interest in it, and it seems to us an extreme affectation of the elite to call it melancholy. He was a philosophical poet in the Petrarchan style, so they say—we do not read his literary works, though we prefer him to Fellini, that filth-mongering son of Rimini, and most certainly prefer even Fellini to this new Sigismondo who had a book published in San Francisco, where they invented this thing, illustrated in color photographs, the book called *The Jane Austen Guide to Anal Sex*—do you appreciate this kind of thing, Signor Del Piero? Do you not marvel at the clothes on the backs of those two? Nothing but Versace for her of the long legs and Armani for him of the body sculpted by Michelangelo. Have you seen them cavort as their predecessors cavorted before them, nude and luscious on the beach in winter?

The pageant they referred to is the historical pageant of Rimini, held once every five years, where the grand prize (King and Queen) is given in the category of *i morti che caminano*, the walking dead. It was awarded to the two newcomers who'd arrived bedraggled just a week before. The prize given for likeness to the historical personages in question and for authenticity of costume—in this instance, determined by comparisons with medallions and paintings—and for "historical wit," in this instance, the mysterious stranger's stunning solution to the meaning of Sigismondo: Sig = signor: Signor Mondo. Mr. World. Yes, he said, I am Mr. World. We won the grand prize: a year in the private quarters of Castel Sismondo.

The story about them I liked best was the story of origins: that they'd come, like the original Malatestas, from the craggy high hills to the west, from a small village that seemed to grow out of rock, and had fallen, fortunately, all the way down, taken all the way down by the gravity of destiny to this city by the sea. (That story ought to have been true.) On the way to Rimini—like the original Malatestas, who began as brigands and thugs—committing all manner of petty crimes, including gifts of the flesh, to sustain themselves until they arrived, like the originals, to take over: not territory, this time, but consciousness. They, the two of them, given the occasion and need, would do anything. They had the need long before I knew them, but I made it possible. The occasion of their final act.

Two months after it was over and I'd managed, with Claudia's merciful care, to drag myself partially back into the light—like the King and Queen, I'd given myself to the desires that belong to darkness—I persuaded Ozaki to come to Volterra to meet Claudia—a scene I had long delighted to imagine: the three of us in the same room; a necessary trio. His first words to her were: "You can't believe how happy it makes me just to look at you." She did not respond and seemed to recoil from his joyful outburst, suddenly unhappy.

On his second night at the villa, as they leaned over my shoulders, I showed them on my computer essential portions of the raw footage. After, she sat quietly—absent, I thought, and for a moment looking like someone else. But who, if not herself? I said I would make coffee. He said, "Okay, big fella"—with total warmth, no irony—"you've done it again. You've managed to create something special without reference to contemporary politics. Jesus! A tremendous stroke of perverted genius. You're one sick fuck, but you've redefined the meaning of avant-garde after twenty years of silence and very little cunning. So where's the dessert? Bring me my seconds along with my first; pile it high on the same plate and take your time out there in the kitchen, big guy, take two hours to brew the coffee, because Claudia and I need to achieve a deeper understanding." His humor brought her half-way back from wherever she was, and I was released, for a time, by the nameless terror that had seized me by the throat. She said, "What kind of people are we who have not vomited and wept from this video? What people after what we have seen can take coffee and dessert?"

◆◇◆

The Grand Hotel. The burly chauffeur leads me to a service elevator off the kitchen—we ride to the top—pass through a door marked NO EXIT—climb a long musty staircase to the attic—negotiate an obstacle course of strewn crates, box springs, and mouse traps—another door—paint peeling—NO ENTRY. He steps aside and bids me enter an enormous suite, featuring a sweeping view of the Adriatic, gleaming floors of inlaid wood, bathrooms tiled in Carrara marble. I'm the fourth guest since its construction in 1933. The first was Greta Garbo, for whom the suite was constructed, so that she might pursue deeper solitude; the second, JFK, so that he might properly console Audrey Hepburn; the third, a figure from the Russian underworld, so that he might entertain an Italian movie star (male), but who was instead met at the door by a fetching female: his assassin.

They were waiting for me, looking expensive; svelte and composed. The impression, which could not have been true—but who knows?—was that these were authentic aristocrats for whom everything had always, and would always, come easily, not excluding death itself. Her English was perfect, with just a hint of seductive accent. Once, in a singular moment of emotion, he told me that her mouth was the forecourt of her heart. About that, he was wrong. She was, I convinced myself, what she seemed to be, though if you could have asked me what exactly did she seem to be, I could not have given, at the time, or even now, an intelligent answer.

The English of so-called Sigismondo was more obviously not native—or if it was, as the gossips had said, then he'd shrewdly disguised the fact. That annoying habit of his of constantly getting idioms comically wrong (the bear who does number two in the garden) struck me as forced—not funny enough—a calculated effort to endear himself to an American bumpkin.

31

This self-named Sigismondo Malatesta was a performance, a series of half-successful gestures, conducted by an unimaginative actor—a performance, nevertheless, that I found compelling. I never knew him. Or do I make the old mistake of assuming his real self to have lain hidden behind the glittering façade? Perhaps that's just who he wholly was: the façade, the performance. I suspect that if I had knocked on his chest, I'd have heard a ringing hollowness within: the nothingness inside, like the volatile propellant of desire, driving him toward the promised end of lasting celebrity, which I—a Dante, he said, for the digital age, for the electronic image—would realize for them in my imminent return to my lost art. (There was something inside him, all right, and I saw it all too vividly.)

"Jack," he says, "you look like something the owl dragged in." (I'd been traveling for twelve hours and hadn't eaten since breakfast.) She says, "Are you intrigued?" In preparation for my arrival, they'd ordered room service for three. I went immediately to the food. With my mouth full, I tried to say, without producing a disgusting sight, "I'm hungry; let's do intrigue later." The mumblings I made seemed to please them. They mainly talked; I mainly ate. He says, "We would prefer to call you Piero, just Piero, after your illustrious predecessor Piero della Francesca, who painted Sigismondo twice and whom Sigismondo brought to Rimini for a year, when Piero was lost in his poverty, as we bring you here, no longer lost, for nine months—how do you like the symbolism?" She says, "Want to give birth?" "You may leave on 1 September," he says. "You may work as you like," she says, "or waste time as you like, until 1 March, when the true beginning begins." (A year later, I learned she was quoting a letter that the historical Sigismondo had written to della Francesca, some 500 years before.) "May we call you Piero, Del Piero?" I reply, "Why don't you try this tremendous gnocchi in pesto sauce? I can't put it all away." (Claudia says that my appetite is a sign that I may be saved, that my mind is not so sick. Is it true? She says the lack of appetite of those two tells her all that she needed to know about *i due pazzi*. From love of food, love of life. It goes without saying.) She, who calls herself Isotta, says, "Good, Piero, tomorrow I wish to give you a private tour of the Tempio after hours, to prepare you. You will find the Tempio irresistible." I reply, "What is this?" "Mortadella," he says. "Do you like this word, Piero?" I say, "When did poor Della die?" She says, "Ha." He tells me that I'll hear, over the next three months, "before the true labor of art begins—on 1 March, dear Piero, that is the date—you will hear many rumors. Make yourself long stories from this gossip, enjoy the stories you make, entertain yourself with them in these rooms in your solitude and as you stroll the streets alone. Because here you are alone, as you have always been. Your humorous talk, can you say it to yourself in your solitude? Can you make yourself laugh, alone in the dark? Have you ever?" She adds, "The humor cannot alleviate. In your solitude, you cannot fool yourself. The humor will stop." "After tonight," he says, "you will see me again one week before 1 March. The next three months will be your proving time. Humor is shit. Humor tells lies because the man of humor is afraid. The proving time commences tonight, after we have left you to your masturbating devices. Time to recontact the self you have lost—to contemplate the work you have always wanted to do. A time for simplification. A time of editing down to the core. A time of concentration and focus." I say, "There is a time for eating, saith the prophet, why don't you eat?" She says, "Shit. Your humor and ironies, like this food, become shit, only much sooner. The shit of your mind. Humor is a testament of triviality, or fear. Which is it, Piero?" "The second bedroom," he says, "with the exception of a simple object, is already barren. The second bedroom is the setting. When we leave you tonight, consider it—as I know you will—you will not take your eyes off the single object: a low table made of

33

black steel, twenty-four inches high and a few inches longer than my bare-footed body. And wide enough. My feet, on 1 March, will be bare. You and your superb technician"—he glanced at her—"will over the weeks that intervene ready the second bedroom for art." She says, "Piero, what is the idiom? I am handy? Yes, I am very handy with my hands, as you will see." He says, "Remember, we—you and I, Piero—shall not see each other until a few days before 1 March; find the purity of the core; become the core; burn all else." She says, "Eventually, if your curiosity about our source of funds is not satisfied, you desert. Seventy-five thousand euros worth of equipment? (One hundred thousand dollars, my friend.) Or this suite? Or your meals here? Or your personal requirements? Or your proclivities? Or our fabulous clothes? How can a tour guide and a bell hop do this? You will believe criminal activity is the source and you will desert, the work yet to be done. Let me tell you," she says, "a true story. To ease your mind." "Then I, too, shall tell you a story," he says, "to arouse your imagination. The body seizes what the imagination lays before it. Hot and quick. The imagination makes us hard." She adds, "Or wet."

Isotta says, "Listen to me: Not long after we arrived in Rimini, three years ago, in the grace period when we were still King and Queen, the boy child of the wealthiest man in the region, who has a finger into this hotel—this boy of seven years was slaughtered—his head run over by a gigantic tour bus in circumstances of ambiguity—some say the wife pushed the child under to punish the husband for an affair. The gossip of the masses is, of course, always a stupid cliché. This man, whom we believe to be innocent of such nonsense, loved and still loves his wife—this wife who took her own life after the death of the child. He came to us and made a proposal. Another cliché, I'm afraid: Such are stories. We had begun our one-year reward of free living in the private quarters of the Castle when he presented himself. As you no doubt have already guessed, he wanted to have a child with me, who he said was nearly as beautiful as his dead wife, whose beauty he could not describe. I did not tell him that the beautiful dead wife is a cliché, and that she is always too beautiful for words. Would Sigismondo permit this? Sigismondo would. He promised an extraordinary reward. He would need to make love to me in the Castle, this was a condition. When pregnancy was achieved—how quickly it was—I was to remain in the Castle until labor commenced, when a team of obstetricians and a mobile, fully-equipped operating room would be sent from Stockholm. Under no circumstances could I leave during the pregnancy—not even for a minute was I to be seen in the streets of Rimini—or the reward would be canceled. No leaving, a healthy child—the gender irrelevant—and the reward would be ours. Why trust this man to keep his promise once he has the child? We did not know the man except for his grief. We took a chance with nothing to lose. If he has the child and does not do what he has promised, we have lost only my virginity. Your ears do not deceive you. My virginity. If he is the honest man he seems to be, then we have gained almost everything. Only when you have completed your work, Piero, shall we have everything. He secured our modest jobs, a lovely home on the edge of town, access to this suite, and meals here at will, as need dictates. And a supply of euros without limitation to be granted upon all reasonable requests. Until we thought of you, then met you in Volterra, few requests, really. He has granted our big request of seventy-five thousand euros for your equipment. This man is good and honest, a loving man despite his wealth."

Then she pulled up her shirt, pushed down her pants to the pubic bone and they were revealed: the ugly stretch marks which I would see once more, on 1 March, in a scene no healthy person would call pornographic.

"My turn," he says. "It is my turn to fill you up." I reply, "Look, the phrase is fill you in, not fill you up." "No, *caro* Piero,

35

this is what we are doing. Filling you up for the long winter nights, when you in vain practice self-love. You are thinking that our names are preposterous? All names are so. Malatesta was itself an invention. Evil head. A nickname given by the enemies of a rough family grabbing for power and then adopted by the family to spit in the face of the enemies, to put fear in their heads by declaring we can embrace your scorn because we are stronger than you. We have the names of our choice. Our so-called real names were choices of others. Did you choose to call yourself Jack Del Piero? The name of a footballer, not an artist. He changed Sismondo, the name of his birth, to Sigismondo and became who he wanted to be: Mr. World. You are thinking this man, me, has no sex with this delicious woman he has been living with for more than three years. This is true. You are thinking this man is an Italian queer, as are so many people of theatrical flair. This is not true. I will tell you a story: He, Sigismondo, at age twenty-six, meets Isotta when she is eleven—not thirteen as the false books say. When she reaches fifteen, the relationship is consummated and she bears him a son. Four years of chastity and pain. On 1 March we will have completed our fourth year of chastity." I said, "But not her. She has not been chaste." He waved his hand in dismissal and said, "What matters is that I am chaste. A woman is by nature not chaste. By reflex." "So you do," I said, "want me to make a raw pornographic film. I don't do that. You know damn well I don't do that." He waved his hand again. "The three of us will make something very rare. *Buona notte*, Piero."

I rode the crowded buses just to ride and drink in the look of things, the tone, the faces: everything about the external scene that wouldn't get into the video. The video would make no reference to Rimini, or any other place.

On one of those rides, I took a seat and wasn't, for once, about to give it up to my elder, because I didn't intend to cling again to a strap with one hand, swaying on the curves and sudden stops, while with the other I clutched my wallet pocket. I didn't care to see myself as another American in suspicion of all foreigners as his moral inferiors. Next to me, standing a few inches away, one of my elders—a category, I've noticed of late, of ever-diminishing numbers. It was my mother. It was no mere resemblance. It was my mother, I tell you. The face and the body type, the dress, the stance, the glasses, the way she wore her hair and the hair itself—the curls—the fragrance of her perfume, the moody ambience of this woman clinging to a strap, looming over me, swaying on the curves—my mother brushing against me—and I don't offer her my seat. I rode that line many times after, hoping to see her and say I'm sorry, Ma, then offer her my seat. She looked the way she looked twenty years ago, of course, before she died, when she was the age that I am now.

I imagine, many times, seeing her on that bus again. I say, I'm sorry, Ma, then offer her my seat. She says, many times, Thank you, Jack, sweetie, but I don't need it, or you.

The voice was flat. "Hello, kid," it said, "I call to inform you that you've lost your umbrella"—and this was my father's way of telling me, twenty years ago, at four in the morning, that my mother had died. He added: "The intercessor has fled." Two days after the funeral—I'd flown back from the festivities at Taormina—my father slashed his throat in the attic, her yellowing wedding dress bloodied beneath him, a note pinned to his crotch: "Shall we tell the truth? The father-son relationship is the original no fault divorce. She was my umbrella. Find your own. Love, Daddy."

✦✧✦

Under my door, on the morning after my first night in Rimini:

Caro Piero,

Following the pleasant meeting last night, we were unable to sleep. Are you truly the necessary artist that we seek? Do you have, as they say in your country, "the balls" for what lies ahead? The tour of the Tempio, which was today to be the inaugural moment of your journey, is not possible. (Does my letter discover you with your hand astroke your penis? Are you wishing it were mine?) Your proclivities—unknown to you— incline to the mediocrity of "normal" life. We propose, therefore, a period of preparation in solitude and denial, a time in the wilderness of your psyche. Think of the days to come as your special Lenten season of fasting. The promised end is not far if you will only renounce some pleasurable act that you, a so-called lapsed Catholic, cannot keep yourself from performing. So long as what is denied has been obsessively indulged. (Are you about to throw away, in sadness, the lubricating jelly you so lovingly apply?) We suggest, in sympathy, that you commit to sexual renunciation and cease having recourse to your secret addiction, what Sigismondo has called your masturbating devices. Since your arrival in Volterra, you have done the good work of abstinence. (We have studied your videos; we know who you are.) In a limited sense, you have achieved chastity. Now achieve true chastity. Banish desire for the peace you seek in the spasms of lonely love. Only you will know if you are faithful to the discipline we set before you. (Possibly I, too, if not Sigismondo, will also know: Expressed semen leaves, about the genitals, a virtually ineradicable bouquet. In my opinion.)

So, then, caro, at the front door of the Tempio we shall meet, dear partners in renunciation. New Year's Day, 2:00 A.M. You have three weeks to prepare the moment.

As ever,

My morning walks that December, beginning at dawn, in cold, fog-shrouded Rimini, were a delight—I walked two, three hours, stopping at cafés and bookstores, avoiding at all times the Tempio and its immediate environs. I was a ghost in the mist and glad of it. After a week of this, I faxed Fred. After much hesitation, I wrote to Claudia. Innocuous messages, really. More or less meaningless. How are you? What have you been doing lately? I'm okay. Here's my address and phone number, just in case.

Fred's first fax was brief: About time, you son of a bitch. I miss you. Claudia's letter—all of them would arrive by overnight FedEx—was not so brief: I am okay too but Aldo has been depressed since your departure. I am told that there is such a thing as an anti-depressant for dogs which is different from the one I must take since your desertion. Aldo does big *merda* on your bed and I am so glad. Fred's second fax: I'm undergoing deep sexual analysis. The theory of my psychobiologist is that I may harbor a female part. I told him the one I'd like to have is clearly not in evidence. Claudia's second letter: I am considering for the first time in seven years a script for a woman my age with the onset of Alzheimer's,

39

who decides to marry Johnny Depp, who plays the role of a poor transsexual who needs my money to reverse his sex change and go back to being a bisexual woman. Shall I take it? In the same FedEx package, her third letter: I am considering selling the villa and moving to London to be near my son, who I did not tell you about. He is your age exactly. Do you object? Which do you prefer? Volterra or London? You must meet my son. Another Fred fax: Don't ask me how, but I know who you live with in Volterra. What are you doing in Rimini, asshole? I'm visiting sooner than you think. Need to lay eyes on the actual Claudia before she dies and no matter what she looks like these days. I fax him back: She looks the same. He faxes: Make an appointment with an eye surgeon or a shrink. Another letter from Claudia: I like writing to you. My answer: Send more letters. I fax Fred: Keep faxing me. Fax me as hard as you can.

After New Year's Day, when I begin to work again, I stop responding, and they do too with the exception of these: Fred: I'll see you in Volterra, where I'll sweep her off her feet. Claudia: Come home, Jack.

One thirty in the morning, New Year's Day—that much is fact, the time, the day—I'm on my way to the Tempio—having consumed no controlled substances with my champagne—keep that in mind—when out of the silence of a deserted intersection they come floating across my path—out of the foggy dark and drizzle and cold they come, astraddle a white bull ox. I raise my hand high in greeting. I'm up on my toes—high bouncing Del Piero—but I am not seen—or perhaps I am seen, but not acknowledged. The white ox halts; jerks its horned head in my direction; nods twice, kindly, in acknowledgment of my dubious presence, while she, in bright summer clothes,

40

who acknowledged little but her own existence, and was not kind, holds the reins—long festive ribbons tied to the horns and tied to the handsome man naked behind her, tied tight about his throat: his eyes shut, head resting upon her shoulders, arms acircle her bared waist—I saw this, I tell you—one hand now inside her skirt—in and down her panties—his fingers—he's fully aroused—he's smiling the faint smile of a lost dreamer dreaming of easeful death—when the wind knifes suddenly deep through my fur-lined leather jacket and the white ox with its romantic burden dissolves back into the silence of foggy dark—but I, who need to dissolve, and fade far away with them, cannot, as sudden clusters of revelers break on through—they rush in clusters at me—they press me—flushed faces press treacherous invitations—I escape them all—turning at last the final corner—entering at last the final space to see her silhouetted there in a square-shouldered, belted long coat, black against the silent vaulting white limestone of the Tempio. I saw her against those sudden dense white stones that dreary night. Where was the white ox? The compassionate and absurdly light-footed white bull ox? She said, with a sweeping gesture, Welcome to my Tempio, while with the other hand touching herself and adding—she caressed herself as she added, My Burberry. Later, it must have been later, she showed me her breast—or was it the breast of the figure in low relief, in the Tempio? A glowing woman, a cold succulence, made of marble. Which woman? My Versace, she said, my Sigismondo, my Ferragamo, my Rimini, my Dolce & Gabbana, my Adriatic, my Louis Vuitton—you, my Piero—as if everything belonged to her, not excluding the sky and the weather, until toward the end of my days in Rimini I had difficulty seeing her except as a mouth, lovely and large—more lovely even than those long legs astraddle the white ox—her skirt far up her thighs—as if everything were destined to end up inside her, to flow in, sucked down hard and fast, who had said to him near the end, "Because I enjoy to swallow,

41

but shall not now my love, or ever, try to imagine it, breathe deep, close your big sad eyes and imagine it, because in the final phase imagination is everything."

I'm trying to remember, not imagine, but probably failing—trying to remember a single night at the Tempio, but I'm no longer sure where to draw the line, believing now there may be no line between what happened outside my head and the dreams and obsessions that anticipated that night, then pursued me, hounding, in the months after—the months in Rimini and the months after Rimini, in Volterra, when I'd returned to Claudia ill, honing in the dark, in my bed, her kind dog curled against me—I depend on the kindness of animals—I honed my obsessions—all the stories, some of them public, some not, of the historical and contemporary Sigismondo and Isotta. I had confiscated it all—dreamed myself into those stories as a player in their sordid and violent dramas—calling my character The Man of Longing—the so-called verifiable facts dreamed, imagined, re-imagined, sucked on like a mother's tit until no more facts except, maybe, the dates of birth and death—until there was only what was inside my head, a monster in there feeding on me, The Outside Man, and on Claudia and Fred Ozaki too, who would bring me in.

As we walked toward the entrance—we had to have walked, you understand, because the white ox was not in view—she said something about how in Italy a man may take another man's arm, or even a woman's arm—should it come to that, she laughed—low, gentle, exciting—in friendship taking his arm, she said, as they walk to the piazza as if you were walking down the aisle to be married. This, Piero, is intimacy without erotic direction. On the other hand, she said—take my arm, *caro*, even though I am not a man—the sex intimacy and the friend intimacy—must one exclude the other? Do they not share the word intimacy? Are you not my friend? So hot to get in? I mean the Tempio. What did you think I meant?

I wondered what, if anything, she wore beneath her Burberry. I thought of the handsome man, at the end denied even her scent on his fingers. I took her arm; she pressed it close; I could feel her, this woman who was the arranger of my fantasy life—who at the end, and for his end, arranged him, *il vero bello*, the truly handsome she called him—that is ascertainable fact, what she did to him at the end.

As if photography of the coffee table variety were about to take place, powerful arc lighting floods the interior as we step in—painful to the eyes. She donned sunglasses—I had none—why would I have taken sunglasses at two in the morning? My chief impression was not of the extravagant chapels, four on either side, but of something at the far end—a feeling of hundreds of meters away—something vague and shimmering at the far end—very far. What was it? I don't believe I voiced my thoughts; it wasn't necessary to do so. That? she said. Oh, that. Only the Church of San Francesco. It was here before Sigismondo created this Tempio, this wonderful pagan blasphemy, but in his mind he was like God before whom nothing could come. Sigismondo, the illegitimate son, named himself Mr. World in order to become the sole legitimizer. This outrageous thing he founded was his world. This temple started there—there was the intolerable origin—there the terrible Before of San Francesco which he needed to make belated. The Church of San Francesco was a cause of vomiting. She points to the far end, more distant now than ever. It had moved, it was moving—the church I mean—as if fleeing her accusing finger—moving to the threshold of nonbeing. This thing of his, this Tempio—he brought them all here—the painters, the musicians, the philosophers, the scholars, the architect, the sculptors, the medallion-designers—*caro mio*, he lavishly extended it from there to here and San Francesco became a mere element of the world he made. I could see it now, the crucifix over the altar shimmering in the distance like a thing shimmering in fierce desert heat—a mirage, disappearing, and in its stead bearing down upon me a woman with flaming hair, head thrown back, lips apart, on a dolphin's back tearing the sea waves. Piero, he had the desire of God because even God feels this unhappiness until he makes a world that comes after, so to think of himself, like Sigismondo, as Mr. World. The God of the Bible is a yearning God, leading a sad and empty life, surrounded by nothing in the absence of time. *Capisci?* Does my Piero think I am mad? The Lord of the Bible and the Lord of Rimini were not truly Lords until they could truly say, I lord it over; they created that saying. I lord it over; I am Mr. Before God. (Am I the village crank of Rimini?) The God who created time, before he created it, imagined down the smoggy aisle of uncreated time—time was just another of his self-amusing big ideas—and what did he see? He saw Sigismondo making San Francesco come after and He thought, I'll do it; I'll create this thing that they will call time. Then they shall be miserable and I at last truly happy thanks to the example of one who will be my creature billions of years hence. Piero, I speak only the normal desire: to come before, to lord it over, to be Mr. World, which the so-called meek of the earth hide in their weak and shitty little hearts.

I begin to walk in deeper. She says, Wait. You have already missed it, they always do—like my tiny Japanese in groups with their cameras. She looks back over her shoulder; I do not track her gaze. My pained eyes transfixed by the wide marble floor—the ochre-colored marble, where light plays over white crests of gentle waves—the little valleys between crests in shadow—like sunlight filtered soft through haze—a feeling of stepping into an ochre-colored inland sea—a feeling of being buoyed up on the swells—a feeling of no terror, though lost to the mainland—and she beside me still, I feel her, who has not stepped in, who is not lost. I cannot speak; my eyes are full. She says, Is the water warm? She says, I do not swim. Now, Piero, turn about because you have missed it.

I didn't turn—not because I might have been thinking—as I think now—the obvious rejoinder to her theological rant: the God of the Bible is eternal; He is; Sigismondo died; Mr. World joined the countless dead in the eternal was. I have no recollection of what it was I thought, or even if what was in my mind could have been called thinking. The Tempio daunted me; annihilated speech and thought, leaving me only my eyes; my eyes became my mind. She faces me; takes my face in her hands—cold hands—and says, Look—pointing to the wall behind me, to the left of the entrance door. I don't react because I don't see it. Like an ordinary tourist, she says, you missed it. She takes my hand; we're dating. We walk to the place and I see it: The tomb of Sigismondo where he lay: 1417–1468. I missed it because it's placed to the immediate right of the entrance door—inside the wall, flush. You enter and your eyes are filled by the splendor before you. Not conceivable that upon entrance you could ignore the splendor before you and glance right, behind you, because you'd have walked in a ways, wouldn't you? It's normal to do so; you'd walk in and it would already be behind you. You don't walk in, then turn immediately away from visual splendor, to see what *might* be behind you in the wall next to the entrance door. It makes no sense to think that you would. Then you'd make your tour; then you'd be exhausted with sensory overload; then you'd leave without ever seeing it there, a modest thing in starkest contrast to the extravagant chapels of Isotta and his ancestors—those exposed arrogant tombs supported by the Malatesta symbol of long life and memory, elephants in white marble. So long as there is memory, she said, he believed that so long do the dead cheat death—the rich and famous who extend their fame beyond the grave are ghouls who feed on our memory. The unknown poor? Remembered eventually by no one except by the Christian God—the nice father—that he never believed in. He took measures to ensure his remembrance. Secular immortality. That is what we truly desire. He had a plan that would survive even the complete destruction of this building and of every building he constructed and of every record or book making reference to such structures. At the end of the tour, can you possibly wait? I will show you and you will understand why you will do with your video camera what you will do, two months from this day.

The extravagant chapels are festooned in morbid blue drapery and astrological images. Railed and balustraded barriers in white marble support sculptures of swollen—I want to say tumescent—children affixed to the top rail—even the females tumescent—entire little bodies blood-engorged. She stands by me—cool, her bearing stiff, unreactive—while the naked swollen children—the *putti*—frozen in dance and play, piping the erotic flute—they appear to move, they bid me follow. She, who had spoken with untoward suggestion in her letter; who spoke to me in the Tempio and after with clumsy insinuation and crudely suggestive prurience—I never believed her to have anything but an abstract relation to those erotic references that spilled and dripped from her lovely mouth—she was a lovely body without heat or moisture, a wickedly crafted manikin, the small breasted Ice Queen—less alive than those vigorous *putti*. Her deepest allure, to which I was not indifferent, was the prospect she held out of sex with the most charismatic member of the living dead. She said, It was Isotta's plan—in his own Tempio to make him inconspicuous. Isotta failed; I will not.

It must have been the contrast between her body—perfect and desiccated—and her low sensuous voice—the moistness, the suppleness of her was there and there alone. That was it. That was the thing that got you—the contrast that made you want to seek hidden treasure, made you believe that if you sought it, sufficiently courted it, and if you were worthy, you'd find it, and it would be unimaginably good. Maybe I thought about it in the Tempio. Sometimes now I think about it. The crude word is the right word.

Fucking her to the rhythm of the swelling sea, buoyed up on the ochre-colored swells. Not her body. Her body wasn't her body. Her voice was her body. In and up her voice. Violently.

I asked about the two intertwined letters I saw everywhere—no visitor could have missed this display of mid-fifteenth-century graffiti. She must have answered hundreds of times as she answered me, with boredom: the "S" and the "I" represent his signature. A custom of the times. According to the scholars. *Et cetera*. The first two letters of Sigismondo. Mark of the ruler. *Et cetera*. But Sigismondo, unlike the scholars, was original in all things. A poet. (Now less bored): It was also a secret sign of his love for Isotta. (Hand to chest. Undoes top two buttons of coat.) The sign of a smitten teenager, "S" and "I," Sigi and Iso, to be read by special readers, like you and me, or by special lovers, extreme lovers. Not carved stupidly on trees inside a heart shape, but in stone. Trees die. (With rising intensity): Do you wish to be extreme, Piero? All real love is so—for a real man. The intertwinement is the double writing of a poet whose signature hides secret meaning. Then she said what no tour guide who wished to keep her job would have said to a normal tourist. This intertwinement is very sexual. Notice how the "S" licks over and under the "I." What is this but the insatiable love of the tongue, his, for her body? She pointed to Isotta's crypt—her hand on my back low, slipping—guiding me to the chapel. Isotta: 1433–1474. No one else had the power. After his physical death she alone determined the placement of his tomb. She designed her own chapel and had it "beplastered"—her word—with more instances of the "I" licked by the "S" than in any other chapel. She willed that those who come after remember his abject love. Down the centuries she would force her meaning—that he—but not she, *caro*—was besotted from the beginning—that he could not lick enough. But she failed because who knows this meaning of the sexual intertwinement except me, and now you? I shall not fail. Three years awaiting the feast of young flesh when at last he filled her, overflowing her banks. Staining floors, hallways, beds—wherever and whenever he saw her—the servants inhaling it in the narrow hallways—the infection of passion—the servants inhaling it—the servants infected and taking each other without regard to the protocols of gender, in the hallways—constantly at work with their semen-soaked mops. A special semen-mopping crew had to be hired. Fourteen years old. Pregnant. This man of undisguised libertinage who always took headlong what he wanted—for her he tied on chastity tight—for her he stored it and stood it for three years. She understood her power. Shall we be brutally precise? She was ten plus a few months when he saw her first, at twenty-seven, and she in her genius foresaw the effect of the waiting and she used it. (Just as I shall use it, she said, to even greater effect.) For three years without the comforts of masturbation—he never touched himself. Finally, free to go in, under her pressure he moved her—the mistress—outrageously the mistress he moved into Castel Sismondo in a bedroom adjacent to that of the second wife—she, Isotta, insisted on the adjacent bedroom. He did not murder the totally shitty first wife according to the malice of Urbino and Rome. But the second one? What choice did he have? Because they both insisted on living there in adjacence and this was a scandal that Mr. World could not take, who gave not a fig for what others said—do you say a fig or a fuck in America? In this country, we call a woman's secret part *la fica*: the fig, the succulent fig. He killed her. Not had her killed. As Isotta watched. I am telling what cannot be found in the books of scholars. Naturally, my middle class tourists, with their mediocre interests, ask about the children. He had many, who knows how many? By wives one and two, by mistresses, by Isotta. Can you say that my Sigismondo and I are not the true heirs of his passion? Can anyone? I answer the tedious questions. I tell them that one

48

of the children likely poisoned her slowly to death. But you and I are not interested in children. (I was.) "S" and "I" were not interested. (I was.) The mission in life of the brats is to destroy the romantic parents, who never wanted these accidents of love. (Was I not once a child of romantic parents?) The little brats scream relentlessly, even when they are adults, because this is what they do: Pay attention to me! Children, at all times, in themselves, are nothing but slow poison. (Was I?)

We moved about slowly—I touched things. She said that I stroked the *putti*, but I did not. She interrupted herself often to apologize for frequently tilting against me. She claimed an inner-ear disturbance caused her to lose her balance, so slightly. I felt the pressure of her body as she talked—I do not believe that she had inner-ear disturbances—my eyes aswim with the surfaces of the Tempio as she moved against me, white marble everywhere. Not the garish outsized chapels but the small sculptures—the low reliefs threatening to pull me under. Undulating stone; glowing fleshlike radiance of polished marble; figures of ribald precocity; I felt a stirring where I had not felt it for some time. I felt her—did not see—felt her glance move down on me. Figures of classical myth—so young and barely covered—carved by magic from knees to navel for the subversive effect of swirling energy—the vortex about the hips. I see them at face level—the swirling middles—males also aswirl—and the words she said unbidden in my silence were—who could forget the phrase?—"female indiscriminate suction." To take the helpless male viewer under, down the erotic whirlpool in this place devoted to remembrance of the dead.

She leads me hand in hand to a special low relief and bids me study. How the sculptor hadn't imposed a conception but permitted her to emerge from under his tool—the fruit of his intercourse with the marble matrix. From the womb of marble; tall, a willow asway in strong wind; hair whipping and flowing; a moving contour seen through water; motion not quite completed—provoking in you, Piero, surprising, lost sensation. Look, she says, the breasts. How small, how desirable. A slight female-roundedness gradually emerging from the boy-flatness of stone. Emerging for you. A young girl's. Is this Isotta? Which Isotta? For the mouth of a lover. Where is he? Are you he? Am I not Isotta? Touch them. Bring your face close. (The flap of her coat pulled back. Then the other flap. Her hand to her breast.)

Across the warm ochre sea to a large medallion set in the wall. The sweeping gesture again—and this, she says, is Sigismondo. We stand before him—his youthful image etched in the glory of changeless metal—more than 500 years later. Beyond time's sadness of ruined frescoes—like the one Piero della Francesca did of him in the Tempio. Free of the sadness of oil paint images altered over the centuries by the filth of insidious chemicals floating in air, futilely restored—re-ruined—by futile desire for the original. Sigismondo in profile: nose alluringly aquiline; strong chin; dramatic high cheekbones; curls over the forehead; the unforgettable neck of him: Drop a plumbline from it to the floor and it defines ninety-degree verticality. You see it in Piero's ruined fresco and in his, Piero's, portrait of Sigismondo—the head shot, so to speak—in the Louvre—and in medallions done by various artists: a neck perhaps never seen in the living world. Do not call it an idealization, she says, because we have no photo or video of him to compare. These medallions, *caro*, he buried them in the foundations and walls of all things he built. When all is brought down—all that is built must fall—these medallions shall be found, immune, in the rubble. He survives all destructions—as we happy three shall survive. His is the last inescapable image—contemplated and held in memory until the last remembering human loses both his life and the God who does not remember, because He does not exist.

As we walked away from the Tempio in the early hours of New Year's Day—a full two months before we were to begin the shoot—she revealed exactly what they wanted to do—assuming I would do what they needed me to do. I have to tell you that without so much as a break in stride, and after a pause that consumed two breaths, at most, I said, Absolutely. Yes. I will do this. You promise, she said? Heart and soul, I said.

A clear, cold morning in Volterra, late November, with snow visible at the higher elevations. We sit outside, by the heated pool, watching the steam rise. Claudia's inside, reading a new script by Roberto Benigni—thinking of making a return—foolishly, she says—to the big screen. Bundled up against the weather, Big Fred Ozaki looks to go about a thousand pounds. He speaks: "Like most Americans, Jack, we're a little retarded." It's the second week of his stay at the villa. He says, "You think I'm funny? A little retarded; you more than me." I say, "I thought Thanksgiving break was only two days attached to a weekend?" He says, "They bend over for me at the college. After the first of the year, I send you back to take over the Program, while I stay here to take over Claudia." I say, "Fred, I'm happy for you." He says, "Remember that Norwegian narcissist with the body nothing at all like she thinks it is?" I say, "I'm not defending her, because who could? But how many of us sport a body actually like we think it is?" He says, "I have no illusions about myself—it's the source of my power over women. Do you recall this Norwegian?" I say, "The English department head with thirty-four essays on the nature of the literary image? Yeah."

Our lounge chairs face each other. I glance left to take in the stones of Volterra—they seem closer and more comforting than ever—or glance right to see, through the glass wall, as I did at that moment, Claudia twisted about in her chair with her legs pulled up under her, script scattered on the floor, gazing back over the chair at the wall behind; chin resting on the harsh top edge of the chair back; lamp turned off; in shadow. Portrait of a Melancholy Woman. Go in and ask. Are you sad, Claudia?

Fred says, "She's brooding in there. As we grow older, we brood more—discipline for dying." I say, "How would you know?" He says, "Jack, what don't I know? Your plan of adding a narrative voice-over to the video will kill the impact of your visual art. This Norwegian genius says to me in the sack, in that whiny voice: 'The central responsibility of the writer, in our time, is to make you see.' I say to her, Elka, do you mind if I come now? Later, I tell her she quoted Conrad without attribution, par for the academic course. I say, Conrad was like you, Elka, jealous of the visual arts. (Elka never comes.) Close your eyes, Jack, Claudia won't evaporate. Okay. RED! What do you see? Don't answer. GREEN! What do you see? Don't answer. Open your eyes. Look at this—points to his jacket. What color is this? Don't answer because who gives a shit what word you might be thinking? Your eyes know what they see; they don't need words: they see. When I said close your eyes and said red, your mind was remembering, but your eyes weren't remembering when they took in my jacket. Your eyes were filled with the present, unlike your mind, maestro, which wandered in the faded past looking for some faded image of red but not this one—unzipping his fly to show me his blazing underwear. The visual image is the thing itself—the word red contains nothing. Fuck literature."

I say, "*Capisco*, but where are you going with this lecture, Professor Ozaki?" He says, "Call me Professor again and in you go fully clothed." I say, "I'd like that." He says, "You and I read the same novel and then agree to meet for beers when we've finished. Why? To discuss. Because that's what you do with literature. You talk about it. But unless you're a tour guide or an art historian—the difference escapes me—we don't talk fatuous talk when we present ourselves to a painting. Maybe an occasional grunt. Because the visual image, *buffo*, is an awesome silence. It demands silence. You're like a woman getting laid. You follow? Under normal conditions, you don't say, Goodness! Gracious! What's in me? Your mind is out of the picture. The frenzy of the eye—the frenzy of the bed. No frenzy? Go read a book. But the fucked up mind can't bear not interfering with the senses—the mind's narrative slash symbolic slash ideological slash etcetera. Its dried-up readings."

I say, "Okay. But what about the book you did on my videos? Answer me that." He answers, "Don't play dumb with me. You know I'm not a visual artist. I'm a talker. A bullshitter of international renown. Visual images—yours especially—are mesmerizing surfaces that hide no depths, that make dialogue and narrative irrelevant, as in screwing. Look at Claudia. Doing what we often do when we read: lifting her eyes from the page and staring off into the room—seeing nothing in the room but what appears vaguely in her mind—trying to make images out of the non-visual medium of the script. The script—think of it like scaffolding. Once we finish work on the film, we remove it. Add the voice-over, you make a piece of hybrid crap. Want to tell stories? Write a novel. Stick with the silent senses, Jack—the mind is a desert."

"When he brought her into the castle," I said, "to live next to the second wife, Isotta was pregnant, and in honor of that he has a medal designed, with the second wife in adjacent attendance. What kind of man is capable of this? (Fred says, I'm interested, but not for the video.) At eleven, the Pope legitimized him, at thirteen a military leader, at fourteen seriously wounded, at fifteen with Florence and Venice against Milan, at sixteen changes his name from Gismondo to Sigismondo and becomes Mr. World, at twenty-seven sees her, the eleven-year-old, at thirty moves her into the castle—the castle replete with his patronage—the lavish meals and furnishings—the poets who write sonnet-cycles in honor of Isotta—this castle of his a little city unto itself, cut off totally from poor Rimini—beset with 10,000 difficulties—the desire is strong to assassinate him, who had surrounded himself with splendor, except in his room—which is spare, monk-like, not even Isotta allowed in there—most of all the death rooms—he loved those rooms—but we don't know anything about the death rooms—I need to make it up. (Fred says, Feel free to invent. You're writing a novel, Jack, about your true heart throb.) What do he and Isotta do between the time that he, at thirty, moves her in, and his death twenty-one years later? Is he bored? Does he still soak the halls with his love? What happens between them, in private? The romance dies? Gets stronger with time? Takes on new mistresses?—soaking floors elsewhere?—while killing all who betray him—the enemies, the so-called friends, the relatives especially without mercy slaughtered. And the Pope condemns him to everlasting Hell in his, Sigi's, own lifetime—making Sigi the first and last human in history while still alive to be condemned to Hell. Are the Pope's charges true? The nonstop fornication with both sexes? Incest with both sexes? Bestiality? Atheism? Nonstop murder? Not to mention the plots to kill all Popes—past, present and future. And other crimes, too heinous to be mentioned. Sigismondo Malatesta, that bitter and violent man who reared in stone his sweetness, his Tempio."

We turn our heads simultaneously to look at Claudia, but she's gone. Big Fred says, "The silent video sufficeth."

III

STILL LIFE

Late on the third day of the shoot, we tried to do something about it. Not for her sake, but for mine—she, as usual, played the role of Isotta the Impervious—played and actually was.

Our first thought was to change the setting of the thermostat to cool and adjust the temperature dial to five degrees centigrade (forty-one degrees Fahrenheit). The result: a steady flow of cold air that lent the odor ever more violent force and slowed the process that we had hoped to hasten. Our second thought was to tape the closed door of the second bedroom—the bedroom of interest. Because, clearly, placing a towel, as we had, at the bottom of the door and stuffing it, as best we could, into the crevice where the door met the floor wasn't working well enough. So we taped, carefully, with duct tape, along all crevices—taped, with utmost care, along the floor at the bottom of the door of interest, using the highest-grade duct tape available in Rimini—we quadruple-taped at every crevice—but it seeped through anyway, in part (but only in part) because cables had to be run under the door; because a cartoon mouse hole had to be neatly sawed from the bottom of the door, to let the cables through; because the taping around the place where the cables emerged from under the door to run unimpeded to my bedroom, my monitoring station, as I think of it, to be connected to my computer—that unfortunate bit of taping could not be executed except in a less than perfect manner. There was no hope. What we did with the thermostat and the duct tape was futile because she insisted on opening the door once daily to get into the bedroom of interest—thereby breaking the assiduously prepared, if less than perfect, seal, at which point the entire suite was insufferably invaded—all my so-called living space was overtaken. On day five I left to take up temporary residence at their house, while the impervious one stayed on in the suite. She withstood the icy suite. She withstood the odor. She slept—soundly, she said—in my bed.

By the end of March, the power of the stench was greatly diminished—somewhat nauseating, repulsive, admittedly, but not unbearable. I moved back into The Grand Hotel in early April, readjusted the thermostat to thirty-six degrees centigrade (ninety-six degrees Fahrenheit), which put us quickly again on track, and she moved back home. Maid service had been canceled in late February—for obvious reasons. When she left, she reminded me, as if I needed reminding, that the sheets I would sleep in were the sheets she had slept in. The first night back I pulled the covers over my head and inhaled deeply, but could not detect her. She had as much odor as Michelangelo's *David*.

I don't sleep well in the heat, and at ninety-six degrees I slept badly for six months, the length of the shoot. At the end of August, I was run down with persistent flu-like symptoms. Claudia's doctor said it wasn't flu. He said that the true cause must have been a mosquito that had gotten into my suite—a mosquito carried to the port of Rimini from a tropical climate. "Because in this manner only, Mr. Del Piero, is it possible that you, who do not share needles, who do not do interesting things with needles, who do not do interesting things with sex—yes? no? yes?—who has had no blood transfusions—thus, my dear fellow, it is logical a mosquito infected your body with malaria. You waited too long to see a doctor: you have chronic sickness." Sounds far-fetched? I'm being treated for malaria; I'm a little improved; I remember, in Rimini, nightly, a buzzing in the dark.

She believed (absurdly) that she needed to get into the bedroom of interest in order to make small corrections in the focus and angle of the cameras, so we retaped daily in March, because of her room invasions—she went in at three in the afternoon and stayed in there—think of it—for fifteen minutes. I'd arrive at 3:15 sharp, to assist in the futile retaping, at five degrees centigrade—we used up a lot of duct tape, I tell you, the store clerk gave me odd looks when I purchased two dozen rolls and cleaned him out—but we taped to no avail. Her daily visits to the second bedroom foolishly opened the entire suite to the blast—for so-called hands-on monitoring purposes—a contemptuous allusion, I thought, to the monitoring that I did, for fifteen minutes, beginning at 3:30. (At 3:45 sharp, I fled.) I saw her on the computer, walking about in there with those long swinging thighs that left no scent in the bed, though I doubted there was anything to monitor—my monitoring station was doing the job—she didn't need to walk about in there. The equipment was of the highest of high-end quality; the focus and angles were fixed; the special light bulbs would last until the next millennium. On several occasions over six months, the security cameras caught her walking briskly in the bedroom of interest—posture pulled together with military severity: a technician concerned with technical matters only, a brisk and efficient professional showing no visible emotion—I believe she had none of the invisible kind either—totally shielded from the appalling final spectacle—only rarely glancing at it. The security cameras saw the key props—the pair of panty hose and the handcuffs—four pair—inadvertently left at the center of the room. We had agreed that they should not be removed. Nor the heap of expensive evening wear.

I get ahead of myself. I'm having difficulty—as you've seen, from the beginning—telling this as a chronological narrative whose set was the second bedroom. Sigismondo insisted on the term, knowing I'd understand and sympathize: "the set." She'd frequently quoted him, who had disappeared early in December, shortly after my arrival, not to re-appear, as promised, until seven days before the shoot, March 1, day of the triggering action. Before he left, he'd given her a single instruction, she said: a directive for "the set." You had the enormous idea, Isotta, the vision of the end, he'd said (she said), but Piero and I have the realizing art, the means of incarnation. Especially Piero. The room, he stipulated, must have the feeling of an ascetic work of non-representational art—geometric abstraction is what we want—all the better to create maximum contrast and highest relief for what lies poignantly at room's human center. I would know how to translate such an intention—he wouldn't be needed until the week before the commencement of the shoot—tech week he called it, when we'd test actors, costumes, cameras, under the lights, go cue to cue, he'd said (she said), though there'd be only one light cue and an untestable final blackout—run quick changes of costume, he said, though there'd be no changes of costume—run sound cues, though there'd be no sound designed in advance of the shoot itself. In the meanwhile, until the commencement of tech week—the term applies to theater, not to film and video, where there is nothing but nonstop tech, beginning to end; but he liked the idea of tech—the words helped him—I'm only guessing—to fill out his sense of himself as a theatrical being, an image for the ages. Who'd want to strip him of the illusion that must have been the basis of his faith? I didn't time it, but I believe that his "tech week" lasted about fifteen minutes, if that.

What he did between the time of my arrival and his disappearance and return was to travel to many walled hill towns of stone, many remote villages, like harsh rocky outcrops, "in preparation." How clean they are (I say he said to himself). He knew that I, "a man of Volterra," as he called me—according to swinging thighs—I, after all, would understand and sympathize—how free those elevated places of the drippings and oozings and droppings of nature, except for the human. There would always, alas, be that, the human, in those thrilling tombs of towns and villages—the unavoidable presence of human garbage, in that clean, clear, cold context. That juxtaposition of human and stony inhuman would be the foretelling image of what was to come, he said (she said). That kind of juxtaposition must be realized in the video. He was traveling to escape the "miasmatic breath" of Rimini. Rimini was swept by bracing sea winds; the air in Rimini was always good. It was the air of the second bedroom—he must have imagined it. In his imagination, he must have been in full flight from it.

He had a plan for the credits. They were to run, she said, as a series of stills, one credit at a time on the screen, each held for five seconds. Thus:

> Woman—Isotta degli Atti of Rimini
> Man—Sigismondo Malatesta of Rimini
> Videography, set, light design—Jack Del Piero
> Technical Assistant—Isotta degli Atti
> A Burly Man

She had selected a title, my dear Piero, with all due respect to your art. *Still Life, A Story of Rimini*. The subtitle would inflect the grand history of the original Sigismondo and Isotta. Would inspire the fanatics—the scholars, the critics, the buffs—to seek out that history as the proper context of understanding for what we will

61

have accomplished. Eventually, the chatter and the video become an indivisible whole, an aesthetic and cultural and historical totality, rolling down the long aisle of time, without impediment. They will publish. They will hold their seminars and conferences. They will bruit us about. And what we shall have done, Piero, the three of us together, will not have been done in vain.

Early in February, a postcard. He was staying the weekend in the haunts of the original Sigismondo's worst enemy—Federico da Montefeltro—in a mountainous corner of Umbria—in Gubbio, a medieval town teetering on the slopes of Mount Ingino, streets dramatically steep. "Hello Hello from the City of Silence. Coffee in deserted and delightful Piazza dei Quaranta Martiri. Lasagna *tartufata, tre volte. Prima colazione: coniglio alla cacciatore.* Wanted you to know." Piazza of the Forty Martyrs. Truffle-stuffed lasagna. For breakfast: rabbit in the hunter's style. He just wanted us to know.

A room, thirty by sixteen, with a ten-foot ceiling. At its mathematical center, bought and mathematically placed by those two: the black steel table, two feet high, six feet four inches long, and wide enough for a body of average width. One body, not two. At one shorter end of the rectangle, a window, floor to ceiling, seven feet wide: a view to the Adriatic and a deserted beach in winter of white sand. Draped. She readily agreed to the purchase of a camcorder to document the extended labor of transformation. From the room as we found it to my desired aesthetic end: the room as proper set of the action.

We remove drapes and rods, fill the holes. At the other shorter end, a door, mid-wall. All walls papered in a gold-flowered pattern, with blue background. After enormous effort, the wallpaper is removed—many layers beneath—how many decades? What did

Garbo see? What did JFK? Down to the original paint: a pale rose. With power sanders the job is completed when a fine smoothness of white wall is achieved.

The electrician removes the antique chandelier at the center, overhanging the table; installs track lighting. Two parallel tracks running the length of the room; four fixtures in each track; fixtures spaced three feet apart and hanging a foot below the ceiling. Between the parallel tracks, over the table, on a separate short track, a fixture hanging over the table's mathematical center; hanging low, four feet above the table's surface and bearing a bulb of hospital operating-room intensity.

We paint to execute my plan for the desired end of geometric abstraction. The two shorter ends of the rectangle—the wall of the window and its opposite, the wall of the door, in mirroring black. Except for the door: white with a vertical black bisecting line, three inches in width. The mirroring long walls feature white fields trisected by black bands two feet wide, floor to ceiling. We do the ceiling in high-gloss black, in contrast to the flat finish of all walls.

The hardwood floor of rich burgundy offends my purpose. The original finish is sanded off (by hand, by Isotta), and refinished with three coats of specially concocted white stain—sealed to a high gloss with three coats of polyurethane. Atop the gleaming white floor, below the radiant black ceiling, the black steel table positioned so that its long sides run parallel to the long walls.

Adjacent to the door, black steel shelving holds the digital recording deck and two servers connected by cables to all cameras and to the monitoring laptop in the other room. Four security cameras: one perched on a tripod at the window, focused on the sea and beach; two others mounted (by Isotta) on the long walls at their midpoint, halfway up the walls, opposite each other and taking in the table and the actors, but not each other.

The main camera is set upon a tripod five feet from the table at its long side. Opposite the window wall, at the other shorter end, mounted (by me) at the very top of the wall, at its midpoint, the fourth security camera. Thanks to its high privileged position, it takes in the other three security cameras, the main camera, the black steel table and what it—the lovely black steel table—bears. It sees all but is itself unseen. It sees the entanglement of exposed power cords and cables that carry the digitalized images. My privileged fourth security camera declares that the image-maker, Jack Del Piero, is also here.

Should the actor on the table wish to lift his head—he did, once, briefly—he sees the window—and through it, the sea and the deserted beach in winter, of white sand.

After day one, she no longer bothered with the two five-pound weights that she'd curled daily, many repetitions, throughout the two-month period of preparation.

Security cameras: footage in black-and-white: A lean man with shoulder-length hair, blue jeans, loafers, black t-shirt, removing main camera from tripod—holding it at his face and focusing on a couple standing the other side of the black steel table, against the long wall. He motions them to step slightly to their right so that the black band is behind them and then motions to make a space between them so that the black band, two feet in width, separates them. They do so. He smiles. Gives them the thumbs-up sign. This is what the main camera sees: Two adults, late twenties, early thirties. He in a tuxedo, a red flower in his lapel; black shoes shined to a glassy finish. She in a custom-designed white gown, spaghetti straps off the shoulders; poured into it; breasts; waist; hips. Movie stars arriving for the Oscar ceremony. Glowing in living color.

◆◇◆

With all preparations completed the week before we were to begin, we had nothing to do but dine at the hotel, at a reserved table beneath the signed photos of diners who mattered most to me: Antonioni, Fellini, Visconti. During the first of nine courses—it was always nine, seven days running—call it the Roman run-up to day one—he, Sigismondo, says, "For the truly fortunate, Piero, life's best end is an important death. Think of Diana, think of Jesus Christ Almighty, think of JFK. The suicide bombers." She adds, "Tristan and Isolde, Paolo and Francesca, but not our predecessors, Sigismondo and Isotta, who died unimportantly." I say, "Isotta, I'm guessing, is the Italian rendition of Isolde?" He, with a sly grin, "Yes, and Isolde expired over the warm corpse of Tristan. Tragic lovers." She: "Isolde was a fool." "Were Paolo and Francesca," I inquire, "also fools?" He: "They were cheating on Paolo's brother, Gianciotto the Deformed, who had sent Paolo il Bello in his deformed place to win her hand. Il Bello was a Malatesta, an uncle, shall we say, of Sigismondo, five or six generations removed. The handsome one, of course, did not tell her that he was a proxy for the ugly one, who was also, do not forget, a Malatesta. The wedding day comes, the deformed one presents himself as the husband-to-be with a hard thing and she assents? Are intelligent people to believe this? After the marriage is consummated, Paolo and Francesca consummate their affair. Gianciotto discovers them at it and with his rapier qualifies them as tragic lovers. This is the story told by Dante and Boccacio. We are sure only of the slaughter—he killed them." She: "Where is the evidence that Paolo was handsome? Where are the photos? The films? In the twelve hundreds, Piero, consider the medical care, the dental situation, the diet. The red meat night and day." He: "Consider that Il Bello was forty years old when they met. In the twelve hundreds, at forty, you are a disaster, my friend." She: "In

65

the absence of visual evidence, why believe the writers? The legends? The camera supplants the word. We don't need the writers." He: "They will believe what you will show, Piero. That we are in truth beautiful people." She, pointing to him, "He is a Malatesta, and the handsomest man in all Italy. And what am I? Chopped liver?" He winks at me. Blows her a kiss. Says: "I am, like all legendary lovers, eager to be deceived by the right woman."

The man strips naked. Tumescence revealed. She strips to bra and panty hose. Removes bra, but not panty hose. Small, full, buoyant, upturned, nipples erect. Main camera goes dark. Security cameras: the lean long-haired man placing the main camera on the tripod; adjusting focus; fixing the angle; the naked man moving to the table; lying on it; lean man gathering the clothes, but then thinking better of it and leaving them heaped where he found them; exits. Main camera: man lying on table; touching himself; stroking; she pulling his hand away; straddling him now at the knees; bending over; taking his penis in hand; stroking: one, two, three, four; bending closer; lips sufficiently apart, but does not proceed to the promised end. Stands. Removes panty hose.

I'm stunned by her appetite. He and I eat half of each course—she all that is put before her. I say to her, in an idiom that clearly neither has heard, "Do you have a hollow leg, Isotta?" They laugh and he says, "Your sexual mind is very interesting." She: "Can you fill up my hollow place, Piero? Can any man? Will Sigismondo? Soon?" He laughs so hard that he cries. She: "In this rare kind of art, which we will together make, sexual intercourse, they say, is necessary." He's convulsed.

She moves up his body—straddling now his thighs. Rises on her knees. Over his thighs but not over his penis. Takes his hands and pulls him up, without visible effort, to her mouth. Tongue in his mouth. Releases him, slowly, without letting go, without visible effort, to the prone position. He's ejaculating—she's sliding quickly down his body trying to avoid the gush, the gushes. She picks up panty hose, wipes her thigh, wipes her pubic hair. Inserts her finger in her vagina. Inserts same finger in her mouth. Finger again in vagina. He opens his mouth as she brings finger close to it, then pulls it away. Tumescent again. Gloriously so. Slides her finger through the small pond on his abdomen. Brings finger to her mouth. Parts lips, then wipes it across his forehead—making the sign of the cross.

He: "No special occasion for her, the way we eat this week. For as long as I have known her—every day of the week such quantities—like this she eats, like a . . ." She: "Say it. Yes. Like a pig who becomes enormous for the purpose of being slaughtered. Beware, my dear fellows, of riding this comparison too far." I ask, "But how do you stay so svelte?" He: "Such a sexual mind you have—are you always so sexual?" She: "I feed my heart, Piero, as do you, on spartan fantasies of a distant future."

She's handcuffing his wrists and ankles to the table's legs. Hard again. He turns his face to the camera—chest rising and falling in deep, slow rhythm. With panty hose she pats dry the sweat on his forehead. He nods. Her mouth is smiling. He nods. Table between her and main camera—she's sitting on floor. Takes his hand and kisses it, open mouth. He turns his head to her. She shakes her head No, pointing to camera. He turns his head to camera. Erection unabated, in the twelve o'clock position. She leans over, kisses him on the forehead, open mouth. Hand on his shoulder: massages, three seconds. With her forefinger touches—one second—tip of penis. His hips rise suddenly—a violent thrust—thrusting—straining—lifting his body from the table's surface. Security camera: Holds the position while she walks around the table, circling many times, as the security camera at the highest perch watches her stumble, almost fall, over cables and cords—panty hose in hand.

He speaks of the course that he and I are about to eat—she's already three quarters through it—spaghetti *alla nursina*—black truffles ground to a pulp, each strand of pasta coated in the thick voluptuous sauce—black pasta—he speaks of it as the proper last supper of a man deliciously condemned. Then lifts his glass and gives the traditional Italian birthday toast: to himself, on his thirtieth. "*Cent' anni*, 100 years. And you, Piero, how old?" I lie; I say, "Forty." She: "You lie. Why do you lie?" He: "It is a good sign. He does not want to die." I reply, "Because it's the one thing truly worth lying about." She: "You must be an atheist—all the great ones are, you know. Your predecessor who painted enormous religious frescoes in Arezzo—did he, Piero della Francesca, believe in God? Don't fool yourself, because he did not believe in art either. Only his own. How else to explain his placement in crowded scenes of a self-representation? He thinks, I shall be kept safe—I shall be cuddled in the gaze of all who look—for as long as there are those who look. You too, like della Francesca, will make an appearance in your art. We say Piero. We say Dante. We say Michelangelo. Unnecessary to say della Francesca, Aligheri, Buonarotti." He: "We say Elvis. We say Mick. We say Ringo." Then he says, "I lied too. Today is not my birthday." She: "Don't change the subject. The subject is everlasting fame. The only true fame—to be known down the endless centuries by your first name alone. How many know who you refer to if you say Aligheri? The scholars, of course. All others know only Dante." "Jack. Jack. Jack," he says. "They will say Jack. Jack's *Still Life*—as they say Titian's *Assumption*, Picasso's *Guernica*." (In my mind I say Claudia.) She: "The world-wide obsession with fame is the deepest preoccupation of atheists. We atheists are in the majority and cannot be sucked in by the shitty idea of Heaven." He: "I will not be sucked." She: "In the days of Paolo and Francesca, and Sigismondo and Isotta, fame in the long time of the world is only possible for the rich and powerful, the secret atheists who commanded the artists and the writers. The poor masses have their shitty Christianity, their lonely obscurity relieved, they think, in the gaze of God." "Don't forget," he says, "the sweet excrement of Islam. Think of the beheading videos. The costumes. The masks. The glamorous swords of olden times. Those who behead are foolishly anonymous, but the one who is beheaded is known. The severed head is held to the camera eye and the world sees down the endless centuries the agonized death mask of a man named Daniel Pearl. The worldwide web. The underground DVDs. He is so familiar: the world knows him now as Danny, as his friends and family knew him. We are all the pals of Danny Pearl. Danny." I say, "Death is not the mother of beauty." He: "Why should Danny have resisted his good fortune?" She: "Sigismondo and JFK—so-called Roman Catholics—think of the parallel. Powerful and promiscuous. The death rooms. Riding in an open car in the city of your worst enemies. Seducers of death—unafraid because they knew, well in advance of physical death, that eternal cultural life was theirs, and this gave the peace that passeth understanding. It is wrong to speak of such people, or the great artists, in the past tense." "Eternal cultural life?" I say. "How about 500 years? How about 2,000 years?" She: "How do you say it in America? Fuck that noise?" He: "The Zapruder film, my friend. This is the model for you. Who was Signor Zapruder until November 22, 1963? Only Abraham Zapruder, a small manufacturer of young ladies' dresses. A Jew in the rag trade, as you Americans say, just a man called Abe until with his camera he also did what Signor Oswald did to the handsomest man of his time. Tell us what he did, *cara*." She speaks with a mouth full of black pasta—laughing—black mouth wide open—she finally gets it out: "He zapped him! Abie and JFK—death-cheaters together forever. But what do we call it? How does the world know it? We say Leonardo's *Mona Lisa*. We say the Zapruder Film. Excuse my French. It was the greatest fucking snuff film ever made." (She eats.) She says, "Your eyes, Jack. (She drinks.) The same as Piero's in his self-representations. Big, deep. His body located in this world, but his eyes, Piero, his sad glittering eyes are fixed on a world elsewhere—behind the eyes. You are beckoned, but not by the world of anemic divinity. You know this—you have always known it. This is why you came to Rimini. (She burps.) Embrace your choice." He: "On March 1, we belong to the ages." I say, "I'm just another camera-bearing atheist." "Not just another, a genius," she says, "soon to be bulwarked against the only death: eternal anonymity." He says, "I lied about my birthday." I answer, "You're repeating yourself." He: "My actual birthday is Christmas Day." She: "This also is a lie." He: "On March 1, from the shit hole of the world's unknown, in the Easter of our art, we are all resurrected. In your case, Piero, as you well know, from the shit hole of minor celebrity. We ascend. The three of us. The newest saints of atheism." She: "This is not a lie." He raises his glass and says, "*Cent' anni* hardly covers it." (She belches.) She says, "They shall kiss our images."

She holds pantyhose before him. He nods. Lays panty over his face, arranging with care, crotch over nose and mouth. Pulls up left breast hard—bends her head down hard to it—tip of her tongue reaching—finding it—licking nipple. Takes legs of hose—wraps each hand twice. He lifts his head—looking at window—sea, beach, white sand. Security camera at window: A couple there, hand in hand, a child romping in the cold March surf. Does he see this? He's hard. He nods. Moves behind his head, sitting on floor, wrapping hose once, twice, thrice tight about his throat. Pressure. Hands, wrists, forearms, biceps. Ten seconds. Her eyes closed. Her lips apart. Her pelvis moving. She rocks back. Her feet in the air. Looking down and in—to her vagina. Thighs—high up—awash. Twenty seconds. Pressure released. A passage of twelve seconds—he's conscious again. He's hard again. Repeat the process. Repeat it. Again. On the fifth repetition, just prior to loss of consciousness, she screams as magnificent jets of semen flash under the lights. Security camera: She comes about—standing now in front of him—begins to masturbate. He watches. Main camera: Sits. Continues to masturbate. She's screaming in orgasm. He's erect again. She's catching her breath, face flushed. She nods. He nods vigorously. Takes hose behind him. Wraps it around his throat. Heavy pressure. Ejaculation. Hold. Hold. Hold. One minute. Hold. Involuntary thrashing: head against hose—legs, arms against manacles—body against his desire. Ejaculation. Hold. Two minutes. Hold. Hold. Involuntary urination. Hold. Involuntary defecation. Hold. Four minutes.

Convulsions of the end.
Eyes wide.
Mouth agape.
Drool drip.

The night before, after dinner, she suggests a quiet bar at the edge of town, where a jukebox plays strictly classic rock 'n roll. She says, "What's your favorite one, Piero?" I answer, "Same as yours. Sympathy for the Devil." He's parking the car. As he approaches, I say, "Let's ask him his favorite." She whispers, "Let's not."

Security camera: The long-haired man, the videographer, moving the main camera and the tripod closer to the body: from five feet to three and a half. Adjusts focus, then angle, then resets speed from normal to time-lapse mode. One frame per minute; one hundred eighty days. Now he's resetting the security cameras to run for fifteen-seconds at fifteen-minute intervals. One hundred eighty days.

The woman places a short microphone stand at the foot of the table. Affixes a short boom—not visible to the main camera's eye—hovering over the corpse, midbody. Tapes a second microphone to the floor where it meets the base of the window.

On September 1, the main camera will yield fifteen minutes of normal time footage—starring both actors—and two and a half hours of time-lapse footage—starring one actor. The security cameras will yield seventy-two hours of footage—featuring the two actors, the finished set, the instruments of artistic representation, one of the actors—the woman—in the role of technician—and a burly man—the chauffeur—with cameo appearances by the artist himself, as he makes adjustments in focus, angle, speed. Do not forget the bumpy camcorder, set preparation footage.

Nothing to do in Rimini until the end of August but check the monitor in my bedroom, which didn't need checking—the show went on. Nothing to do but walk the streets which I'd walked too many times. Nothing to do but observe her entering the room of interest, which didn't need entering—whose sealed door I didn't want breached for the reason you understand. Nothing to do but fend off her frequent invitations—subtle, crude—to share her bed. I feared her—for the reason you understand—though I wanted to go to bed with her as much as I wanted anything before.

From late April through the end of August I traveled, returning to Rimini on alternate weekends, for the weekend, to assure myself that all was well with my project and that she—preposterous anxiety—hadn't changed her mind. I traveled much in the paths he'd taken in the weeks prior to his ecstasy. Like him, I was a man for the rocky villages and the walled hill towns of stony purity. A man of Volterra. To Gubbio, then, my first excursion—to Gubbio in order to partake of what he partook of: lasagna *tartufata*. (Am I a ludicrous pervert?) Fred said it was like the moment of consecration in the Roman Catholic mass—the hushed partaking of the symbolic body and blood of a man who called himself Sigismondo Malatesta. He then stood at poolside in his vast body, made rapid signs of the cross in the air, and mockingly intoned: Take this lasagna. Do this in memory of me.

Not only the hill towns: Venice, Rome, Milan, Palermo, Taormina. In those places, long ago, they knew me well. Now they know me not. (Get thee behind me, Satan, I know thee not.) My anonymity, painful as it was at the sites of my former renown, did not curb my appetite. Even for Italy, the meals were improbably good. Claudia says that though my way is not the way of the saint in the desert, eventually my love of food—even bad food—brings me to God. I tell her I'm a confused ascetic. "No," she says, "only confused." She's patient, but not eternally so. She says it twice, "Not forever, Jack."

Arezzo in early July and my body doing penance—chills, fevers, night sweats—Arezzo, where I'd gone to see della Francesca's great frescoes, *The Legend of the True Cross*, and then left, my fever not slight, for an hour-and-a-half drive through mountains on winding narrow roads, alongside of which I saw them, standing, in groups of two, three, smoking, sometimes singly, waving to me—women in tight short pants, exposed deep cleavage, soliciting passing drivers—it was no fantasy of a heated brain—on steep narrow roads getting into parked cars and trucks that stuck out into my lane—on their knees I saw them—on all fours like dogs—on the way to view my predecessor's *Madonna del Parto*—the pregnant Virgin Mary, in the small town of Monterchi, a tiny museum there housing a single painting, that of the Virgin who Isotta said had never been penetrated except by her finger, as this painting shows—traditional long blue dress—open at midbody—Mary's long finger, "the correct finger," she said, "in the opening—the opening so shaped as to resemble, as you say in America, a slit, her slit, Jack, can you speak this word?"

In the shadow of the museum of the pregnant Madonna, at an open-air restaurant, under a dark haze of buzzing flies, they served me the only dish on the menu: *Pernici alle Olive*—partridge with black olives—in sage, olive oil, red wine—wrapped in anchovies and prosciutto. "They say," Isotta said, "that Piero modeled his Madonna on his mother. Others say Isotta. You are thinking your mother. But she resembles me, does she not?" I couldn't keep the flies from my partridge. If partridge it was. I ate with gusto. Shivering. Later, back at the hotel, in Arezzo, I took two cool baths, but it didn't help.

THE AESTHETICS OF LIVIDITY

Postmortem: One-six hours. Window camera: bright deserted beach, gentle surf, gulls. High-perched camera: handcuffed corpse on its back; corners of room in light shadow; a rectangle of sunlight between corpse and window, sliding slowly duskward. Toward window. Out.

A woman enters. White tank top, black leotard, barefooted. Surgical gloves. Walks around the table—stepping with care over cables, pushing hair behind her ear. No expression. Nothing to express.

Main camera: skin blisters; staining on body's dependent areas: vivid bluish-red. Also thighs, hands, neck. Observe the dense clusters of pinpoint hemorrhages on abdomen. Note the rim of lighter color—heartbreaking pink—along margins of bluish-red zones. Stagnant blood, under gravity's spell, creates the body's last palette.

The woman undoes handcuffs, jerks body onto its side: its back to camera. White patches of skin where shoulders, buttocks, and calves had pressed the table. This is the art of vascular blockage: White islands in a blue-red sea. Woman pushes corpse to its former position. Exits.

Window camera: lone man in winter coat, staring seaward, motionless. Mike at window: windblast. Mike over body: silence. He's still a handsome man.

My symptoms were chronic: four or five days in remission, though weak, followed by a day or two of fever and night sweats, and weaker still. I traveled on. There were times in July and August when I was confined to my hotel bed: better there than Rimini, where the shoot ended, finally, on August thirty-first. I called Claudia and asked if I could come back. She responded, after a significant pause, "As soon as you can." I returned the next day in the same grueling way that I'd left. Three trains, two buses, in the midst of an episode of whatever it was I had. When I step off the bus in Volterra, in the warm rain, she's there. At the villa, she takes me to her bed—"because it will be easier to hear you in the night"—I was glad of it, but did not give myself away—then she called her doctor who would come the next morning. I awoke twice in the dark, quietly—I was not in trouble—her breathing a little too quick and not deep enough to indicate sleep. Aldo stirred, but did not move. I said her name. She did not respond. I reach under her night shirt and touch her. Lightly, slowly: breast, belly, abdomen, thighs. How warm she was. I slip my fingers under her panties. She turns and hugs me fiercely. She said, "*Voi stare con me? Vuoi fare l'amore? Con me?*" You wish to be with me? You wish to make love? With me? I responded, "*Non ancora.*" Not yet. She said, "*Hai paura, Jack?*" Are you afraid? I said, "*Sì.*" She said, "*Non hai paura. Forse domani. Forse l'anno prossimo.*" Don't be afraid. Perhaps tomorrow. Perhaps next year. "*Non importa. Perché tu sarai per sempre qui.*" It doesn't matter. Because you will always be here. "*Nel mio letto.*" In my bed. I could not speak. She kissed me on the mouth; I could not respond.

In the year since I've returned to Claudia, Big Fred has made several extended visits to Volterra—"because I can"—"because it's a thrill"—because he needed to bring the news, in person, to see the look on my face when he told me that my colleagues, by unanimous consent—and with a stunning show of love and respect—had successfully carried the argument to the upper administration that my twenty years of uninterrupted service constituted a de facto grant of tenure. "Congratulations, Jackster. You now have something to fall back on—a bed of thorns—if you don't fall soon and forever into this woman's unimaginable bed. Shall we cut to the chase? When was the last time you had honest dialogue with your dick?"

He had unlikely strategies for urging resolution in favor of the Claudia option—as he sat by the pool in the warming weather, poured into a Speedo bathing suit barely visible owing to the cascading fat of his belly and the elephantine love handles about the hips and back. He begins by saying, "I know exactly what I look like at this moment. Do you acknowledge what the mirror mirror on the wall is saying to you?"

Fred: No offense, but you're going saggy under the chin. Unmistakable in profile. Undisguisable. In the absence of ocular proof I would guess in addition the onset of radical failure of the pectorals. Radical. Normal at your age. You get tits. Never as big as mine, but who does. What are you? Fifty-eight? Sixty-three?

Jack: Fifty, you bastard.

Fred: For purposes of civility, I accept that figure. A modest collapse in the buttocks. Am I right? You walk away from the bed after a roll in the hay and this is the spectacle that she must endure. I haven't seen it. Neither, I speculate in all sadness, has she. No offense, but where do you get off?

Jack: Where do I get off what?

Fred: Claudia, that's what. Think I don't know your thoughts in that quarter? Let's cut to the chase. A little tire around

77

the waist. A man of my massivity and renown, no problem. A tall drink of water like you? Jackie, tell the total truth. A little ass-collapse? Have we cut to the chase?

Jack: Your point?

Fred: Claudia, that's what. She's changed. You know and you do not know. You're half-living in another world. You, not Claudia, are half-dead.

Jack: No slippages for you?

Fred: These days I come only three times per encounter. Nonetheless, women continue to sense my power. I'm dying, hombre. How about you? Coming? Dying? Cat got your tongue? I say Claw-dee-uh. You say Claouuu-dee-uh. The first syllable in your mouth is endless. In your mouth, she's the Italian mouthful, God bless her. Has she been in your mouth? It's an incantation. You say Claouuu-dee-uh and up she comes before your eyes as she was in her early films. How do you summon the one who's already here? This is a major fucking paradox. Who do you live with, Jack? Why aren't you banging her? Because you can't bang the woman who's not here, that's why. Or have you gone gay on me?

Jack: Who says I'm not?

Fred: Gay?

Jack: Banging her.

Fred: Her eyes, that's who. Kid, you never stopped traffic, not even twenty years ago. So what are we talking about?

✦✧✦

After the doctor left, and the pharmacy had delivered the medications, I moved to my own bedroom and fell into dreamless sleep. In the late afternoon I awoke to find Aldo standing by my pillow with a piece of stationery in his mouth, which he promptly let fall on my face:

Caro Jack,

If you wish to be healthy—do you wish?—you must do these things. If you will not do these things, then you must go back to America. *E poi, tutto é sciolto.* And then, all is lost.

1. Before breakfast: take Aldo to pee.

2. After breakfast: wash the dishes.

3. Before lunch: take Aldo to do *merda*.

4. After lunch: take a nap on my bed with me. *Capisco, senza toccare.* I understand, without touching.

5. After nap: sweep kitchen floor and dust.

6. Before dinner: take Aldo for pee and play with him for half hour with toy rat.

7. After dinner: wash dishes.

8. Before sleep: Brush my hair slowly for fifteen minutes.

9. Make bath for me. Spy on me bathing through door a little open.

10. Go to sleep in your own bed, but no more with Aldo.

THE MAGIC OF RIGOR MORTIS

Postmortem: twelve—twenty hours. High-perched camera: Woman enters. Same costume. Hair tied back. Applies fresh lipstick. Yawns.

Window mike: Thunder. Window camera: lightning in a darkened sky. No rain. She stands at the groin. Standing by her man. Main camera: dried crumbly appearance on belly, thighs. A memory of orgasm. High-perched camera: Woman removes one glove and with bare forefinger wipes tip of penis and scrotum several times. Wipes finger across black leotard at genital area. White, viscous. Postmortem extrusion of fresh semen. Wipes finger across corpse's lips. Does not kiss its soldered mouth. Pats corpse's shoulder, kindly. Exits. Rain spatter at window.

High-perched camera: Woman enters with burly man. The chauffeur. He's carrying two straight-backed wood chairs. Tape measures corpse's length. Places chairs about six feet apart. Woman and burly man—one at shoulders, other at feet—haul corpse to chairs. Head only on one chair. Feet only on other. No sag. Not a trace. Corpse returned to table. Exit.

Main camera: Writhing of feet: thirty minutes. Arms jerk—spasm—spring up at elbow—freeze off table. Goosebumps: legs, arms. New stubble on heretofore clean-shaven face. A fashionable mode of young male appearance. Not a bad-looking man.

On one of the days when I feel too weak to perform my ten enjoyable acts of redemption, Claudia takes me inside a closed room in a remote corner of the villa—difficult to walk about in—the floor covered with teetering stacks of papers, drawings, watercolors, notes—*Cara Mamma, ti amo*—school tests, amateurish models of churches, houses, prehistoric beasts, rocketships. The accumulated expression of a child from his second year through high school—Valerio, her son—she'd kept it all—to throw away one piece of paper would have been the same as throwing herself away. "When he created these things, Jack, a great joy, but as he grew older, a great grief to look at. When he was seven, to look at what he made at four—a sadness too much to bear." I say, "But you see each other?" "Yes. An international business man, living in London. Three or four times a year. Not always Christmas with the grandchildren. When I was young and working, I had such excitement for the world—the world was close—the world was many times inside me like a lover. I had no fear. When I was young and working, I filled this house. Now only myself I fill. The world has gone away with Valerio and here I am in this villa where I look out at night and see only myself in the dark glass. How many times I go to another room to get something and when I get there I don't know why I went. Even if you stay I don't know if together we can fill this house with good feelings—or even the bad ones together with the good ones and the boring ones."

I tell her that we need immediately to make another list with just one thing to do on it. A list for the two of us. To organize Valerio's room. Organize chronologically. Make categories. Organize chronologically within the categories. Buy boxes. Today, not tomorrow, buy the boxes. Put section dividers inside the boxes—to create levels of personal history—the deeper the earlier. Label the boxes. Create an exhaustive inventory of the room so that if you want, you can quickly find Valerio at two and seven months—box three, level five. An inventory so detailed you don't need to go into the boxes. We reserve one evening a week for it. Stretch it out to the end of time. She says, "If you want, we can do this." I say, "Let's go buy the boxes." She says, "And the tape." "The marking pens," I say. She says, "To work together to the end of time."

The Valerio project, shopping for groceries with Claudia, my daily rituals of redemption, dubious experiments in cooking—so I filled my days. That spring, with some improvements in my health, we would drive over to Volterra in midafternoon for long strolls in the freshening breeze. Claudia wanted to show me how wrong I was. "Look, Jack," and she'd point out boxed shrubs and flowers in bloom and dwarf trees boxed before café entrances. "Look: What do you call that? Gray-orange? Gray-brown? The buildings are not all gray as you say." I ask, "Why don't you wear the big floppy hat and the big sunglasses to disguise yourself from the public?" She responds, jauntily, "I am as you see me—in disguise from the woman in '8½'. "

Our conversation flows easily, until awkward silences, without warning, trap us in downward glances of embarrassment. Can we live with what I did in Rimini? Do I stay, or do I go back to Connecticut?

PUTREFACTION (1)

Postmortem: One-three weeks. Main camera: Distended abdomen. Grotesquely bloated face and neck. Who is this man? Dark discoloration of lower abdominal wall invades chest, neck, and face. Display of deep arborescent red on thighs, chest, shoulders: the image of trees in winter. Window camera: Gray sky, deserted beach, a single gull. Main camera: Green overtaking red. Scrotum: Size of a cantaloupe. Protrusion of eye globes. Protrusion of swollen tongue. Purging of urine, feces. Bloody fluid from mouth, nostrils, rectum. Microphone over corpse: the slow leaking of a balloon—like the music of flatulence—like the sound of sighing. Skin slippage at feet: an effect of loose, falling socks. Slippage at hands: a glove-effect. Who is this man?

High-perched camera: Black-and-white tones, stark. Woman enters. Same costume with addition of surgical mask. Covers mouth but cannot suppress vomitus. Gags. Spits. Exits. Window camera: A single gull diving into the sea.

We were walking Aldo. Big Fred grabs my arm, stops and says, "Wait. Don't move. Conceive of your ideal venue as one of those classic old movie palaces in New York and Los Angeles. I'm thinking the silent movie era, 1926. Here's the thought: Here and there, but never in moments when your mikes pick up actual sound, you run the old-time silent movie piano accompaniment. See where I'm going with this? One of those bad upright pianos somewhat out of tune. You alternate the trembling melodramatic chords—the girl tied to the railroad tracks—that kind of thing—with the frantic funny stuff—the music falling over itself—the notes tumbling pell-mell all over the place in a riot of comedy. Think of the dissonance. Image versus music. The reviewers can't handle the complexity. You become a cultural icon—a figure loathed and praised." I say, "See what Aldo just did?" He says, "What?" I say, "Aldo peed on your leg."

PUTREFACTION (2)

Postmortem: One—six months. Main camera: Blue-red, then green-red, then forest green, then black-green, then black. Thoracic and abdominal walls suffer total breakdown. Visibility of viscera. Finger- and toe-nails loosen, drop. Window camera: Sunbathers, a topless woman, gulls. Main camera: Liquification of soft tissue. Audible puddling and dripping from table: consistency and color of cheap olive oil. Drip. Total liquification of viscera. Drip drip. Total skin slippage. Total hair slippage: head, pubis. Scalp slippage. Brain paste. Solid organs on view: black mush. Prostate, last bastion of his manhood, alone resisting decomposition. Window: Children nude at water's edge. A bald head flashes in dark deep water. Teenagers of both genders practice soccer headers. Gulls. High-perched camera: Woman enters, masked. Removes mask. Wipes drippage with mask. Brings mask to face. Inhales. Exits. Main camera: Final liquification of soft tissue. Ligaments, tendons: black wires. Window: Big-bellied couple power-walking along water's edge. Kites high, brilliant. Gulls. Main camera: Suet. Fatty waxy substance at buttocks and extremities. Suet. High-perched camera: Woman again: soup spoon and small jar. Stirs fatty liquid. Spoons into jar: What she'll have in place of ashes. Suet. Suet and bones. Skeleton emergence. Prostate at last liquefied. Window: Twilight: Gulls. Gulls. Gulls.

I'm slouched far down for a long hot bath in her tub—on a fine April morning—in another season of chastity in Volterra—my head alone above water—my severed head afloat—when I hear it—a blast that rattles the window. In panic I rise and look out to see a woman and a big man—Isotta and the chauffeur—disappearing down the slope of the olive orchard and I race—dripping, naked—to find her on the terrace, cursing, ejecting a spent shell from a pump-action shotgun, placing a new one in the chamber. She looks at me with a look I'd seen only once before in "Once Upon a Time in the West"—oozing sensuality and surprising rage. She says, "That woman wants something from you. *Quella puttana!* I say to her, Wait, I will tell Jack that you are here. When I return I have this and I say to her, Is this what you want? I would like to serve you a special meal if you come back. I will kill you both, especially you I told her. Maybe you are hungry now, I say? I will kill you now, I told her. They run and I point this to heaven and I shoot. If they come again, *Signor Artista*, you can make a video of their brains in the swimming pool." She smiles. The normal Claudia returns: "Ah, You are ready to swim with me without clothes. *Finalmente.* You have become excited down there." (My hand a sudden fig leaf.) "Don't be shy, I have seen that little big thing before." The softness in her manner disappears just as suddenly as it had intervened: "Bring the computer to me now." I turn and she giggles as I walk briskly

84

away. "And the two backups, Jack." I slip on her robe and bring what she's requested. She points the shotgun at the slope. I carry computer and backups to the edge of the gorge. I'm in her thrall. She says, "Wait. Go back. Open it." I comply. "Come back. Have you used one of these?" I replied that I'd done some hunting as a kid. Leads me to within five yards of the computer. "Shoot the computer." I look at her. "Shoot the computer." I shoot the computer. "Again." I do it again. "And the backups. Four more times." I shoot the computer four more times—the final blast sending the last vestiges of the Rimini video tumbling into the gorge. "The evil you hide inside your miserable machine, *dov'é andato*?" Where did it go? I reply, "*All' inferno, speriamo.*" To hell, we hope.

She sits at the apron of the pool. Face in hands. Sunlight weaving her hair. Rises, grief-struck. Comes close. Opens robe: "My robe makes you hard?" Her eyes are full. A gentle laugh: "Two times a week I wish you to wear my clothes." Her hand. We kiss. My finger. I spread the robe next to the pool and we make love. After, we swim and make love in the warm water. I can't tell you what it was like. It wasn't like anything. She said—during—"Oh, God." I remember that clearly. "Oh, God." Or maybe it was me who said it. She says, "It was you, Jack." I remember that I kissed her as we made love. Later, as she ties my hair in a ponytail, I'm aroused once again. I say, "Possibly tonight?" "No," she says, "not tonight—now. Quick!"

I made love to Claudia Cardinale. I finally made love to her. And fucked myself over while I was at it. Between the desire and the spasm, no thinking intervened. My work was gone.

That afternoon, strolling in Volterra—take my arm, she says, and I do—we're surprised by a sudden shower over the mountains. After some minutes, drenched, we find a café beside a florist to take coffee in silence, until she says: "Your face tells me that you are not here." I respond, "I'll be back in a minute." She says, "Your voice is dry." When I return, I give them to her—her hair wet, her dress damp and clinging, her arms full of hyacinths. She says, "Thank you, but you have not come back. Are you sad because you cannot give what you receive?" I say, "I think I'm coming down with a fever again, that's all it is. I'm cold." We walk out into the piazza—clouds gone, her hair long to the waist, my self-possession guttering.

Back at the villa, she says, "If you truly loved me I would tell you to hold on tight and you will be safe. Take my hand, I will show you your fear in a handful of pictures." We're in the library. She takes down three books and an album. Arranges them in a line on the long table. I said, "When you made the ponytail did you notice how my hair was growing thin?" She replies, "How could I not?"

IT'S A WRAP (1)

Postmortem. August 31. Window camera, mike: White sands hidden beneath a blanket of skimpily clad bodies. Sound of surf overpowered by human din. High-perched camera: The mass of cables and cords, the boom over the table, the three other surveillance cameras, the ascetic beauty of abstract design, the decedent in post-putrefaction: fully skeletonized except for some patches of white substance along hip bones. He's acceptable again.

Woman and burly man enter, bearing tools and garbage bags. No surgical masks. She in shorts, plunging halter top, running shoes. Work gloves. He in jeans, t-shirt, running shoes. No gloves. He sneezes. Wipes nose across forearm. They exit. Return with broom, whisk broom, mop, pail sloshing water, shovel, cleaning supplies. A brief exchange of inaudible dialogue. He shrugs. She gives him a saw. He picks at his crotch. She takes a hammer. Pushes hair behind her ear. Nods. They begin.

✦✧✦

I tell her I must sit; I'm not well. She leads me to the couch and wraps me in an orange and brown afghan and then brings the books and album to the couch. I know those books; I can imagine what's in the album. She turns up all lights to maximum intensity. She says, "Look at me. Are your ears bad? Look at me. Who do you see?"

Jack: Claudia.

Claudia: Which Claudia? The one you carried to Volterra from America? If you see me on the street and have not been introduced, who do you see?

Jack: Claudia.

Claudia: Look at me.

Jack: I just did.

Claudia: Again. Do not turn away.

Jack: I didn't turn away.

Claudia: You did.

Jack: I see Claudia.

Claudia: You are a little crazy. Because if you pass me on the street and do not know me you do not stare. You do not want my autograph. You do not turn around and say to yourself, Who is that woman? Who is this woman so beautiful? This you do not say in your mind. You see only an old lady, well-preserved, nice clothes, who goes to the health club three times every week. We do what we can.

Jack: You're still—

Claudia: *Silenzio!* I am still? What is still? I am not beautiful in
           the way you see in pictures. But not looking *come una
           strega.* Like a witch.

(Jack smiles. Takes her hand.)

Claudia: You look good, Claudia, the butcher says. I say to the
           butcher, When do you say you look good to people
           twenty-five and thirty-five? I am still means I am old.
           I am still means I am not still. *Capisci, buffone?* Do you
           understand, clown?

Jack: I never passed you on the street when we were strangers
           and I do know you. Why should I respond to specula-
           tion?

Claudia: Why should you respond to truth? Better to live in old
           movie? You are pretending to be innocent at fifty-five
           years old.

Jack: I'm fifty, Claudia, as you well know.

Claudia: You worry about your age? (Opens album.) Who is this?
           (An infant.)

Jack: It must be you.

Claudia: Why do you say must?

Jack: Obviously there is no resemblance.

Claudia: Is the ceiling of this room so fascinating that you must
           look at it?

Jack: Obviously you don't look like this infant or a twenty-five
           year-old, for that matter. Is that your point?

Claudia:	Have I resemblance to the young person in "8½" who makes you sing like a poet? Like a boy of eighteen who is in love for the first time?
Jack:	We don't need to proceed with this little drama. Does it amuse you? How long have you and Fred been planning this little event?
Claudia:	Aaah! He is irritated! But why? All the time you were in Rimini, I plan. This is not drama. Look at me. Who is this? (A child of perhaps eight or nine.)
Jack:	You. I don't recognize you, but you. Because why else would you show me this picture? Can we stop this?
Claudia:	We will not stop. Does this child look like the baby?
Jack:	Yawn.
Claudia:	What? Be careful: I have a shotgun.
Jack:	No, she does not.
Claudia:	And this one? Who? (A girl of perhaps sixteen.)
Jack:	I want to say I recognize you, almost.
Claudia:	What does it mean you want?
Jack:	I actually do not.
Claudia:	Does the teenager look like the girl? Or this old lady next to you?
Jack:	Not in the least.

(She closes album and opens book of photos to the *Esquire* shot of 1961. The one if you look at it while standing you are in grave danger of sustaining serious head trauma when you crash to the floor. The photo which, if you are sitting, you get a head injury, nevertheless, for life. She touches his forehead and says, No fever. You are only a little sick in your mind.)

Jack: I don't feel well, Claudia.

Claudia: In your mind. Did you fall down and hit your brains when you were young?

Jack: I've known that photo for years.

Claudia: Ah. You fell down and hit your brains when you were young. You know this one as Claudia? Forty-five years ago? You see me?

Jack: Absolutely.

Claudia: And this one? And this? And this one? And this? These so-called goddesses of sex and beauty? Claudia all?

Jack: Yes. Four times yes. Claudia all.

Claudia: Look at me. Please. This last one you say yes. Look at the teeth.

Jack: What?!

Claudia: They have already at forty-two years old become too long. Gum disease. My idiot dentist. Look at my teeth. (Pulls up lip.)

Jack: We needn't go on with this. I know you've changed.

Claudia: Do you like my teeth? Look. (Pulls up lip.) Do you love my teeth?

Jack: Can I go to bed now?

Claudia: No. These bombs of sex look like me? You need a doctor for your mind.

Jack: You've changed a little.

Claudia: A little?

Jack: Not a little.

Claudia: We are progressing. Bravo. Do you enjoy this not a little change?

Jack: Who likes to grow old?

Claudia: The physical troubles, nobody. But I do not look in the mirror and mourn. Jack, why do you mourn for me?

Jack: You write a little drama to teach a lesson. Lessons are boring, especially in theater.

Claudia: You are not bored. You are afraid. This is not theater. This is here. You are not here. *Guarda me!* Look at me. Who do you mourn? Me? You? Both?

Jack: Between the pictures of the beginning of your life and those of your movie star days, let's call it your middle years, I see no connection. None. Satisfied? Between the pictures of your movie star period and you who . . . (looks away) no connection. Okay?

Claudia: This woman who is not at the beginning or the middle, who you do not look at, where is she if not at the end? In the last phase?

Jack: You're not at the end.

Claudia: You agree I am not at the beginning or middle?

Jack: What choice do I have?

Claudia: We are progressing nicely. You are less crazy.

Jack: Where are we going?

Claudia:	I do not choose to be at the end, but I am at the end.
Jack:	I don't want you to be at the end. Or in the final phase. I don't want any phases.
Claudia:	You are a child. When you say "you" which "you" do you speak of, *caro mio*? The movie star? This is the phase you want, yes?
Jack:	All the Claudias.
Claudia:	I never looked like the pictures. My eyes always saw someone else, even when I was young. I thought I looked strange. Not beautiful. The photographers, *caro*, are devils. Fellini was a marvelous devil.
Jack:	We made love in the full light of day. Twice. In the sun. And again tonight. With the lights on. Have you forgotten?
Claudia:	I will never forget. (Long pause.) But in your mind (points to *Esquire* photo) it was this me you made love to. Not this me. (Touches her breast.)
Jack:	You can't know that.
(No response.)	
Jack:	You can't know that, damn it.
Claudia:	What does you can't know that mean when you say it two times so angry?
Jack:	I made love to all the Claudias. I love all the Claudias.
Claudia:	You want to love this old lady. But you do not love her. (Gently:) Because you do not know how to love?

Jack: Do you love me, Claudia?

Claudia: I want to love you.

Jack: But you don't.

Claudia: We don't.

(Long pause.)

Claudia: I wish to give you a picture, tonight, of me ten years
            in the future, when I reach seventy-eight. If I live. If
            you stay with me.

Jack: I'll stay and take your picture at seventy-eight.

Claudia: You must go.

IT'S A WRAP (2)

The woman smashes at the base of the skull. The burly man saws
the rib cage. Head skitters across floor. Feet smashing. Leg sawing.
Pelvis smashing. Elbow sawing. Garbage bags. Scraping. Sweeping.
Spraying. Washing. Table polishing. Two large bags. Not full. Twisted
and tied. Garbage. Man exits with bags. Woman at window. Man
returns. Gulls scream and wheel—swoop and skim low—alighting
on water. Man and woman gaze at window. Another great day for
the beach.

IV

RECOGNITION

Claudia decides to sell the villa and move to London—to become a full-time grandmother and embrace the final phase. Then Big Fred arrives for his last visit—this time to stay at the villa—an invitation, he assures me, bespeaking the inevitable: that I am out and he is in. I have one option: to return with him to Connecticut and resume my duties at the college.

Not even he could truly lighten the tone of things that week. On his first day, he declares, "Intimate revelations are quivering on the horizon. Spare me, dear friends. I know the score." One morning, Claudia proposes that we visit Volterra's main tourist attraction: the Etruscan Museum—a warehouse of literally hundreds of burial urns and chests, richly carved with scenes of sensual delight. Fred insists we take a vote. The result: three nays. I note in him an uncharacteristic undertow of sadness. When I mention this, he says he isn't sleeping well. That's all it is. I reply that I'm not buying it. He says, "Dude, you're sad; she's sad. Why would you think I'd mourn my best friend's terminal loss?" That is the second time I've heard those words in my lifetime. First from Claudia, then from him: best friend. Don't remember if I said those actual words to them: best friend.

A subject of brief comic relief is supplied when the Volterra weekly reports that Sigismondo's tomb, after five hundred years, was opened to satisfy the scholars and the forensic anthropologists. Hitherto unknown facts are established: He stood at five feet four; the right arm, the one that carried his terrible swift sword, was longer than his left; he wore his hair in bangs—as portrayed in various portraits and medals—apparently to cover a small excrescence of bone. The art historians are quick to compare facts with della Francesca's paintings: the nose was more aquiline than Piero had represented it; the chin, in reality, less strong. The chin was weak. Claudia shows us a book containing a photo of Piero's fresco in San Francesco. She says, "This is Piero's joke on his vain patron. Look. The two dogs. If you make them stand on their back legs next to him, he looks like a dwarf."

The Sigismondo discussion gives Fred an idea. In the service of history and forensic anthropology, we are obligated to establish the truth of Claudia at the time of "8½." Would she cooperate in this intimate inventory? She would. Waist? Twenty-three and a quarter. Now, she says, twenty-six. Height? Five feet six. Now, she says, five feet five. Breast? Thirty-eight. Now they have fallen—she touches her knee with a grin—and measurement makes no sense. Hips? The same. The number? "I do not wish to say because I always wanted to have smaller hips." Fred insists we need to measure the length of her arms, legs, the circumference of her wrists and head, the length of her neck. She says, "Why not?" And we do. Then Claudia pulls her hair back: "How do you like my ears? They are like jug handles, as they say. When I was acting in 'Big Deal on Madonna Street,' they pinned them to my head. But my funny ears, my deep-set eyes, and the corners of my mouth, which turn down—a director said this downturn was the secret of my erotic force—these facts will not be found if my grave is disturbed—which it will not—five hundred years from now. Only the form of my skeleton remains, which has no erotic force. And then, at last, I will be loved for who I am." A moment of unclouded laughter, all around. Fred looks at me and says, "What an excellent woman, you fool." She reddens.

"Claudia," he says, "there's a photo of you in which you lie naked from the waist up, your back alone—what a shame!—exposed to the camera." She says, "You want to ask me about the moles?" He says, "What else?" She replies, "The five moles on my back? Black? Why didn't we cover them with make-up?" "Or have them removed," I say—possibly too eagerly—"by a dermatologist, because it's no problem to have this kind of blemish removed, if you consider it a blemish." She says, "Do you consider it a blemish, Jack?" I answer, "No, of course not." "What's your answer, Claudia," Fred asks? She says, "My answer to you, Big Fred, is why don't I have plastic surgery to lift my face and Botox and surgery to raise my breasts?" Fred replies, "I'm in love." I reach under the table and take her hand. She places her other hand atop mine. Fred says, "If you need privacy, this is what a bedroom is for."

On that desperate afternoon before his last night in Volterra, Jack Del Piero says, "How can I? I'm virtually broke," and Fred Ozaki responds, "But I'm not," as he flashes a wallet heavy with credit cards. Big Fred's goodness enables Jack to assuage (a little) his desperation and purchase at Volterra's finest men's shop a smashing black, pin-striped suit (Armani: 1500 euros), a formal white-on-white dress shirt (Versace: 100 euros) a grey tie (De Sanctis: 100 euros) and a pair of black dress oxfords (Bruno Magli: 400 euros). Because he intends to present himself properly appareled. Because he wants to dazzle her. Because he needs to be shut, for good, of his solitude. In the presence of a third party, a witness, Big Fred himself, he intends to propose marriage. "Should she refuse you," Fred says—"which she definitely will—you have a costume for the exit scene of your coffined life—and I'll be there—I promise—to admire your stylishly attired corpse."

That night, Jack shaves and showers for the second time. Brushes and flosses again—flosses too hard, drawing blood. Then splashes, too generously, Fred's cologne on his face, neck, wrists. From the garden, a white flower for his lapel and a single blue flower—symbolic color of the Virgin Mother, Fred remarks—to present to her in temporary substitution of a ring. At 11 p.m., with Fred in tow, he's about to knock on her door when he remembers and returns in a cold sweat to his room—Fred in tow, Fred laboring to breathe—to swab out his ears. Another hopeless glance in the mirror. What is to be done about my face? Nothing to be done. Checks his hair for the fortieth time—his coiffeur, she'd called it—using now a hand-held mirror for side and back views, when, Jesus! he spots it, under the lower lip—Jesus—the emerging pimple. Nothing to be done. Probably not noticeable anyway in her softly lit bedroom. Down the corridor again, Fred laboring in bathrobe and pajamas. Light from under the door—she's talking to Aldo. Jack knocks.

She appears in pink and green pajamas decorated with rabbits and bear cubs. Big Fred huffing, scratching beneath his robe. Jack with a forced frozen grin. Cologne reek. Blue flower held out—Jack Del Piero like an idiot from a novel by William Faulkner, minus the drool. What Claudia sees and what she hears, as Jack speaks his prepared lines like a bad actor, is cruel farce: mockery of her thwarted desire for love and mockery of the pain she thought she'd kept so well-hidden—even, almost perfectly, from herself.

Jack (mechanically—in fear): As Fred Ozaki is my witness, I have come tonight . . . As Fred Ozaki is my witness, I wish to say—

100

Claudia (cutting him off): Good night.

(Fred enters room and sprawls, scratching, on love seat.)

Jack (still in doorway): As Fred Ozaki is my witness, I wish to say, Claudia Cardinale, will you kindly marry me?

(Silence)

Jack: Will you marry me?

(Silence)

Jack: Marry me, Claudia.

Fred (yawning): The kid is afraid. Give us the comic ending, sweetheart.

Claudia: As Fred Ozaki is my witness, I do not wish to marry you. *Buona notte.* Or to live with you. Everybody is afraid. Including our mothers and fathers. Good night.

Jack: Why not marry me? You love me, don't you? I know you do. Don't you love me? Say it.

Fred: Our revels now are ended. (Scoops up Aldo and leaves.)

Claudia (two inches from his face): You know nothing.

Jack: Say you love me, Claudia.

Claudia: I love you.

Jack: Marry me, then, since you love me.

Claudia: No. (Gets into bed. Jack sits beside her.)

Jack: Marry me.

Claudia: Please. This is too hard.

Jack (taking her hand and putting it on his crotch): This is hard.

101

Claudia (pulling her hand away): What's the matter, little boy? Mommy and Daddy didn't love you enough? You want to fuck your Mommy?

Jack: What?!

Claudia: Or me when I was twenty-one?

Jack (smiling): Well . . . when you were twenty-one, I was four.

Claudia: A difficult choice?

Jack: What can I say?

Claudia: You want to have my moles removed?

Jack: I never said that.

Claudia: But you thought it. Because you fear to touch them?

Jack: I never said that.

Claudia: Because you fear to touch them?

Jack: Maybe. (Pause.) Yes.

Claudia: Do you know me? Did you truly think you could win me with these clothes like an oily Italian producer? You think I care about the clothes you wear? Your cologne stinks like a funeral parlor.

Jack: To honor the occasion, that's why I bought them. For respect.

Claudia: No. To hide.

Jack: Stop it.

Claudia: I have just begun. When you returned from Rimini, I failed you and myself. Because I feared to be alone. I should have said a man who does what you did I cannot live with. Yes, I love you. Yes, I want to make love to you, even now. Tonight. No, I will not. Because love, Jack, it conquers nothing. A man who does what you have done . . . how do you live with yourself? You knew what they wanted and you did what they wanted. With your camera looking at the beach, and the painting of the room, and the camera showing us the wires and cables and other cameras—this intercutting with the corpse—ah! You are so modern. Most of all with your clever cameras you wanted me to say, as you want the world to say, *Ecco un' artista!*

Jack: Yes! I want the world to admire who I am: *Son'artista!* Yes.

Claudia: It is art to film murder?

Jack: It wasn't murder. It was assisted suicide.

Claudia: *Merda!* Art is magic. Art is illusion. She killed him.

Jack: But I didn't—I did not.

Claudia: Without you, no death.

Jack: I didn't kill him—I recorded it—I was only an objective observer who did not interfere except with his cameras and set painting to raise what they did to the level of serious art. I'm a creative documentarian. But so what? I went along with you, didn't I, when you asked me to destroy the computer?

Claudia: Because you were afraid of me or the police?

Jack: I think I'm innocent.

Claudia: You think? I feel dirty because I did not throw you out as soon as you returned. Do you feel dirty?

103

Jack: I told you I wasn't an actor in what they did.

Claudia: You have no horror in your heart?

Jack: I have inexplicable fevers. I might have guilt, I suppose.

Claudia: You suppose?

Jack: I created a terrible beauty—that's what I did. That's what I confess to. Why should I restrict my material?

Claudia: You are calling this poor insane man, who was killed, material?

Jack: The artist, as artist, is beyond good and evil. (Pause.) Isn't he? (Pause.) Am I not?

(Silence.)

Claudia: You killed that man.

Jack: I'm a cold-blooded monster?

Claudia: You are very confused. *Ed anch'io*, who went along with you for so many months. No more.

Jack: How can you love me?

(Silence.)

Jack: At least that, I have. Your love.

Claudia: What do I have?

(Jack is speechless.)

Claudia: This obsession with my old movies and the black-and-white photographs, I know what it is. They give you feelings of mourning—you love your feelings of mourning—they make you feel good, these feelings. You love your feelings of mourning more than who you mourn.

Jack: I love *you*. Cut me some slack.

Claudia: Loneliness is better than to be with someone like you.

Jack: After I destroyed the computer we made love for the first time—in living color. That tell you something? Loneliness is not better than love. Nothing is better than love. (Pause.) Someone like me? I'm *that* bad?

Claudia: Jack, you love an idea in black-and-white. We made love because after two years of chastity, explosion is inevitable.

Jack: You're hurting me.

Claudia: It is necessary to hurt you: You are the pornographer of death. The living of this world do not appear to us in black-and-white. Look at me—I am in color. (Turns his face to her.)

Jack: They happen to be your most beautiful pictures. They do the most justice. The ones in black-and-white. That is the only reason. (Looks away.)

Claudia: Those pictures are the tomb of a young woman no longer here. The movie in Rimini and those pictures are the same. They are tombs. You are the tomb-making artist. You love me young and dead, safe, unchanging in a black-and-white picture, never to be touched or made love to, but not who I am, a dying old lady who does not want to die, who loves life, with liver spots on her hands—look—and loose skin under the chin and here on my arms. Look how it

105

sways, this skin, when I move my arm like this. Look, my tomb-lover—are you alive?

Jack (Looking away): I think I'm not the man you need me to be.

Claudia (fiercely): You know nothing.

Jack: I'll change.

(Silence)

Jack: I'll change.

(Silence)

Jack: I know I can change. (Pause.) Say something.

(Silence.)

Jack: Aren't you going to say something?

Claudia: Yes. (Pause.) Go back to America with Fred, a wonderful friend to you. Now leave my room because near you, my love, I die faster.

(A knock. Claudia says, *Vieni*. Fred enters with the whimpering Aldo. Fred says, He doesn't like me.)

Claudia: *Tu mi capisci*? Jack? *Amor mio*?

Jack (leaving, turning at the door): If you . . . (leaves).

(Claudia turns out the lights. Silence in the dark.)

On the last morning, as Fred hauls luggage to the taxi, we have a final moment. I say, "This is wrong." She says nothing. I request her London address. She only says, "Goodbye, Jack." A tender hug, and that was it.

Milan to Boston: side by side in first class. Fred bought me the ticket, so he said. About forty-five minutes into the flight, he tells me it was Claudia who purchased the ticket. She didn't want it revealed, but he was revealing it so that I could plunge to the bottom of my grief. I say, "Thank you, Big Fred." We eat and drink, especially Fred. At one point he sings softly, sweetly, in his rich bass: "Who can explain it? Who can tell you why? Fools give you reasons, wise men never try. The tremendous wisdom of pop culture, Jack. What can she possibly see in him etcetera. The question of reviewers and other fools of reason. For you, love at first sight. The first sight of an image, years ago. For her? Possibly the curious consequence of a brain lesion."

I say, "Fred, how are you feeling? Feeling okay?" He replies, "I'm feeling jubilant. You destroyed the computer and its treasure, but I've got notes and I'm going ahead with the book. They'll say I made it up, but so what? If we're blessed by God, we get fired for moral turpitude. Then Italy requests extradition on charges of accessory to murder. Larry King calls."

About an hour from Boston, he says, "Jack." Takes my hand, says "Jack," then slumps forward. I cannot wake him. The steward calls for a doctor, if there is one on board. There is. She comes. Checks his pulse. An extended effort to revive, but Big Fred Ozaki is dead.

I live now in the house he willed me, where I summon my familiar ghosts. Mother. Father. Fred. The man who called himself Sigismondo. All the Claudias. Word has it that students and faculty in the Program have enthusiastically nominated me for a teaching award. I'd be proud to win one. And I've begun, strangely, to invite colleagues over for dinner—seems as though I've lost my scorn, as she'd hoped. The dinners are a hit. I find them only semi-bearable, but do not intend to cease extending invitations.

You might have guessed it—I have a dog now. Wash dishes, sweep the kitchen floor, walk the dog—these acts comprise the deep structure of my days. The anchor of my evenings is this: Before turning in, for fifteen minutes I brush my dog's coat. I'm a failed conjurer—Claudia does not appear. Around midnight, it's lights out and instant sleep—only to awake, often, shivering with fever in the dark, to brood until dawn—on the compelling woman I knew in Volterra, on the man who could not love her, and on the woman I live with now—inside moving images—forever young.

Special thanks to the videographer William Noland, of Duke University; Dr. Kim Panosian, Medical Examiner for the city of Elmira and Vice President of Medical Affairs at St. Joseph's Hospital, Elmira; and the writer Barbara Kremen, who encouraged a final rethinking of a difficult passage in the narrative.

Fiction by **Frank Lentricchia**